Murder by Mishap

by

Suzanne Young

Sybown Press

Cover Designer: Jamie Reddig

All rights reserved

Copyright © 2012 by Suzanne Young
ISBN 978-0615622866

Sybown Press
9028 West 50th Lane, #1
Arvada, CO 80002-4441

Dedication

This book is dedicated to my siblings
Richard
Elaine (in memory)
Carolyn and
Joshua,
with love.

Other books in the Edna Davies series

Murder by Yew, 2009
Murder by Proxy, 2011

Chapter One

"What's that glittering in the middle of Peg's garden?" Edna Davies muttered to no one, as there was nobody nearby to hear.

She had been walking to the Providence Art Club to attend a special exhibition of watercolors and oil paintings by students from the Rhode Island School of Design when, passing the home of a friend, she was momentarily startled by a bright reflection. Only seconds before, she probably would have passed it by unnoticed but for the sun taking that moment to slip out from behind dark clouds to spotlight the object.

Ordinarily, she wouldn't have taken that route to her destination or been on foot at all, but an early April, blinding downpour had forced her to pull her car to the curb a block away. Over in minutes, the storm had left behind an invigorating, spring freshness to the air that prompted her to leave her car and walk the few blocks to Thomas Street and the distinguished art club.

It shines like a diamond, she thought, approaching the wrought-iron bars of the tall fence enclosing her friend's property. Pushing her face against the metal, Edna strained for a better view. Wanting to get as close as possible, she removed her brushed-felt hat and squeezed her head through the bars.

Getting a better view, she saw what looked

to be a brooch sticking up out of the soil. Only a small piece of the edge remained caught in the dirt, so the pin was propped at an angle. Apparently, the rain had washed it enough to allow the sun to reflect off the stone's facets. She could now see that the object consisted of more than a single diamond. The one that had sparkled, catching her attention, appeared to be the center stone of the brooch. Encircling this main diamond were sapphires which, in turn, were surrounded by smaller diamonds and an outer ring of rubies. A lovely red-white-and-blue pin, lying atop freshly turned earth about three feet from the fence.

Peg must have dropped it, Edna thought as she felt the first twinge in her spine. When she tried to back out from between the bars, she found it wasn't as easy as it had been to slip her head in through the rain-slicked metal.

After a brief struggle, her ears began to sting from rubbing against gritty iron. She grabbed hold of the shafts a few inches above and to each side of her head in an attempt to relieve her aching back of some weight. She considered her situation. While she was thinking about how to extricate herself before her back gave out entirely or her ears became bloody, a pair of brown brogues beneath khaki pant legs stepped into view.

"That you, Ed?"

Recognizing the distinct Rhode Island accent of her former college roommate and long-time friend with a mix of relief and embarrassment, she said, "Yes, Peg. It is I."

Edna thought she heard a stifled snigger.

"May I ask what you're doing?"

For nearly fifty years, the two friends had communicated by understatement, each attempting to outdo the other with dry wit. Hence, Edna's reply, "I've been admiring the brooch you've planted in your garden."

"Shall I call Stephen and have him bring the camera?"

"I would appreciate it if you didn't," Edna said. Before she could say more, she felt the hem of her dress brush across the backs of her thighs as a gentle breeze picked up. Reaching behind with one hand, trying to make certain her skirt was in its proper place, she asked, "Am I drawing a crowd?"

"Not yet."

"If the wind gets any stronger, I will be, I fear."

"Instead of mooning my neighbors, you could have come into the yard, you know. The gate isn't locked."

"I was on my way to the Art Club when your old pin there distracted me. I hadn't planned on staying this long."

"What pin?"

"It's a bit to the left of your foot."

"Oh, yes. I see it." From her nearly doubled over position, Edna saw only Peg's hand as her friend picked up the jewel. A brief pause preceded a sharp intake of breath. "My god. This is Mother's brooch. She lost it ages ago." After another few seconds of silence, Edna heard Peg mutter very softly, "My god. Poor Cherisse."

"That's nice, Peg. I'm very glad to have found your mother's jewelry." She winced as she felt a jab of pain. "I don't know about your 'poor Cherisse' but do you suppose you could help me get out of here? I think my back's breaking."

"Oh. Yes. Sorry, Ed. I think it'd be best if I came round to your side."

"Okay, but please hurry." Edna grabbed the bars on a level with her shoulders, managing some relief on her spine. She heard no footsteps on the sidewalk from Peg's rubber-soled shoes, but she knew her friend had arrived when she heard muffled giggles.

"Oh, Ed, I wish you'd let me get Stephen and the camera," Peg's voice broke through her laughter.

Peg was the only person in the world whom Edna allowed to call her "Ed," mainly because she'd never been able to break her friend of the habit. Now, Edna assumed her coldest tone. "If you do, I will seriously consider ending our friendship."

"Perhaps you won't mind if I call the gardener over to help. I see he's decided to get back to work. Fortunately, he finished plowing up this patch before the rain came. Imagine you finding Mother's old pin in the dirt."

"Yes, Peg, but I'm fast regretting it. Please get me some help."

"Right. Sorry, Ed. Hello! Goran! Over here, if you have a minute, please."

Another pair of shoes came into Edna's view. These ones were worn, black work boots accompanied by dark blue pants with mud-spattered cuffs. "Yes, ma'am? What seems to be the trouble?" His voice was low and soft, carrying only a hint of amusement. Pleasant, Edna would have said under different circumstances. Now all she could think was, *He's about as funny as Peg. Isn't it obvious what the trouble is?*

"Edna, I'd like you to meet our new gardener, Goran Pittlani. Goran, this is my very best friend, Edna Davies. She's just found my mother's long-lost, birthday brooch. See?"

"Peg," Edna almost shouted. "Show and Tell later, if you don't mind."

"Yes. Of course, Ed. Goran, would you see if you can help me to free my friend from these bars? Perhaps not, but it's worth a try. Otherwise, we may have to cut them."

Edna felt Peg's fine-boned, delicate fingers prodding and pressing her ears tightly against her head as a larger, stronger hand pushed gently on the top of her head. On Peg's command, Edna pushed against the bars with her hands at the same time as she arched her back and, finally, pulled her head free. With a groan, she turned and sat down heavily onto the narrow grass strip that ran between the fence and the sidewalk.

Peg leaned down to take her arm. "I think it would be best if you came into the house. The neighbors might think you're a bag lady, sitting here on the street."

Edna was certain she heard another suppressed chuckle. "You may be right, but at the moment, I can't stand upright and I'm wondering if I'll ever be able to wear pierced earrings again."

"Can I be of any more assistance, ma'am?"
The gardener's deep voice came from behind
Edna.

"I think we can manage now. Thank you,
Goran," Peg replied. To Edna, she said, "Try
standing. For me. The ground is wet and you're
liable to catch your death, on top of everything
else." Peg tugged gently on Edna's arm and
between her pulling and Edna pushing up with her
free hand, she managed to get to her feet and stood
only slightly bent over.

In this manner, she hobbled beside Peg,
around the fence, through a narrow pedestrian
gate, up the brick walk and into the old
Graystocking family mansion. The front door
opened into a large, high-ceilinged foyer. Opposite
the entryway, a wide staircase rose to a landing
from which stairs branched both right and left to
the second-floor. An enormous crystal chandelier
hung in the center of the vaulted ceiling and
sparkled in the light from a window in the hallway
that ran above the front door.

On the main floor, to the left of the stairs,
the door to the library stood open, revealing a
wide brick fireplace. A matching door to the right
of the staircase was hardly ever left open and, as a
matter of fact, was always locked when the office
was unoccupied by the master of the house. Wide
arches at the left and right of the foyer led to the
dining and living rooms, respectively.

Having been to the house many times over
the years, Edna sensed more than consciously saw

the interior because, immediately upon entering, she collapsed onto a Persian rug immediately inside the front door. She rolled onto her back and the hard surface made her feel better immediately. "Be a dear and straighten my skirt over my legs, would you?" she said, looking up at Peg.

Her friend obliged before pulling over a straight-backed chair to sit beside and look down at Edna. There was a glimmer in Peg's light-blue eyes and her voice held only a trace of mirth when she asked, "Comfy?"

"Very. Thank you." Edna closed her eyes. "I'll get up in a minute, but this feels too good right now." After an unusually lengthy silence, she opened her eyes to see Peg studying the newly-found pin with an uncharacteristically somber look. "Your mother's, did you say?"

"Yes. Father gave it to her for her birthday the first year they were married. Her birthday was July fourth. That's why the red, white and blue. He had it specially designed." Turning the jewel over in her hands, she looked down at Edna. "The pin in back is bent, but other than that, it doesn't seem any worse for the wear. I think it can be easily fixed."

"What did you mean when you said 'poor Cherisse'?" Edna remembered Peg's mother's name had been Isabelle, so who was Cherisse?

As Peg returned her gaze to the brooch, her eyes took on a faraway look, and instead of answering, she seemed to drift off into thought.

After nearly a minute of watching and waiting for a reply, Edna broke the lengthening silence. "If the clasp is damaged, the brooch probably fell off when your mother was working in the garden, don't you think?" More memories flashed through her mind. "As I remember, she was often tending beautiful rose bushes along that side of the fence."

"Mother loved roses best, I think. At any rate, she spent more time in that patch than in any of the other gardens. The smell of roses still takes me back to my childhood. We had vases full, all over the house." Peg's face brightened as she smiled. "There'll be rose bushes along that entire stretch again. I've decided to put the gardens back the way Mother had them. I should never have agreed to turn everything into lawn when Joey and I were married, but then we traveled so much, there just wasn't time to work in the yard."

Peg's face seemed to soften when she spoke of her first husband. Just as quickly, the look disappeared as she tightened her fingers over the pin. "I was cleaning out the closet in one of the back bedrooms this winter and found an old hat box pushed way back on the top shelf. It was filled with photographs, mostly black and white that Father must have taken because Mother was in so many of them. Looking through those pictures and seeing the joy on Mother's face, even when she was working in the kitchen garden, made me want to restore everything. Stephen agreed it would be a good project for me, since he's been increasingly tied up with bank business lately. As a matter of fact, it was he who found Goran to help me. Goran's been preparing the beds. I wonder why he didn't see this. It must have surfaced when he was tilling." She took the brooch between thumb and forefinger and held it up to the light from a fan-shaped window above the front door.

"I suppose turning the soil brought it to the surface, but it must still have been covered with dirt. The morning's cloudburst washed it clean," Edna theorized. "Luckily the sun struck it just as I was passing or it might have gotten stepped on and buried again."

"What is today?" Peg looked down, frowning in thought for a second or two before answering her own question. "April twelfth. Mother lost this brooch on April fifteenth, the year I graduated from high school, so that was, what ... almost exactly fifty years ago." Peg raised her eyebrows as if amazed at the coincidence.

Edna was about to ask how Peg remembered the exact date and who was this Cherisse person, when she heard a door open and the sound of footsteps crossing the foyer.

"What's all this?" a male voice demanded above Edna's head.

Chapter Two

Edna felt Stephen Bishop standing over her. She would have to tip back her head in order to actually see him, but she refused to strain her neck or her back to do so.

"Hello, Stephen," she said, looking at Peg.

"Edna? Margaret?" He spoke their names as questions.

The women looked at each other for several seconds as Edna waited for Peg to say something. She suspected Peg was waiting for her to speak.

Stephen Bishop was Peg's second husband. For the past two years, ever since Peg's wedding, Edna had been trying to figure out why she couldn't warm up to the man. She didn't think it was solely because she and Albert, her own husband, had been close friends with Joey Luccianello. Edna hoped she and Albert were more charitable than to resent Peg's remarrying, but Stephen was as different from Peg's first husband as two men could be. Joey, impetuous and easy-going, had almost never been serious. Stephen, on the other hand, was perpetually solemn. In fact, Edna couldn't remember the last time she'd seen him show much emotion—no joy or sorrow, no hope or despair. She wondered again what her witty, fun-loving friend saw in him.

Joey had been a speculator. The only son of wealthy parents and youngest of three children, he had been pampered and spoiled by both his parents and his older sisters.

Stephen was an only child, as Peg had been, but came from a poor family. Struggling to bring himself up in the world, he was now majority owner of a small, private banking establishment. Stephen's first wife died the year after their daughter graduated from college and left home for a job in New York City. He'd been married and widowed twice since then, having lost his third wife the year before he met Peg. Edna and Albert had wondered, only between themselves, of course, if the wives had all died of boredom. On a more somber side, they rarely mentioned that each wife had been extremely wealthy, a circumstance that had allowed Stephen to achieve controlling interest in the bank.

"Ladies?" His insistent question broke into her thoughts as he moved into view on her left. Peg, still sitting in the chair to Edna's right, looked up at her prim husband.

"Ed's hurt her back. Lying on the hard floor is making her feel better. She'll be up in a minute or two, won't you, Ed?" Peg glanced back down as she spoke.

Catching the twinkle in her friend's eyes and the quiver of her lips, Edna felt like a mischievous school girl again and was horrified to realize she was about to burst into a fit of uncontrollable giggles. Peg apparently saw the signs herself for she turned away, looking over her shoulder toward the dining room.

"I found a brooch in your garden." Edna

would have explained further, but for a sudden, sharp pain just above her knee. Had Peg kicked her?

"Really?" The single word burst with interest, unusual for Stephen. "A brooch, you say?"

"Just an old thing Mother lost years ago," Peg replied, cutting her eyes at her husband before frowning down at Edna and giving an imperceptible shake of her head. All Peg's gaiety was gone, replaced by ... what? Was it worry? Anger? Fear? The look vanished before Edna could decide.

"May I see it, Margaret?" Stephen held out a hand, palm upward. It was one of the things Edna disliked most about Stephen—his insistence on always using his wife's formal name. *No give to the man at all*, she thought, watching the exchange between husband and wife with growing curiosity. They were acting almost like strangers. She lay still, waiting for the scene to play out.

Peg displayed the pin in her palm, but out of her husband's reach before she tightened her fist around the jewel. "Father had it made for Mother's birthday. I haven't seen it for fifty years, so I'd like to keep it with me for now. A day or two," she added, as if in compromise.

"You know I like to keep our valuables at the bank. I want to ascertain if that piece is too expensive to be lying around the house."

"Of course I won't leave it 'lying around'," Peg snapped, her eyes flashing.

At that moment, the sound of someone

clearing his throat drew their attention to the front door. From her vantage point, Edna saw a man who looked to be of medium height, although from floor level, she found it hard to tell exactly how tall he was. What wasn't hard to determine was that he had a sturdy build and a thick mop of brown hair. Dark brown eyes stared boldly from beneath fine brows and his face was clean-shaven. From the mud-spattered, navy coverall he wore, Edna judged that this was the gardener who had assisted in her rescue.

"'Scuse me, sir," Goran Pittlani spoke in his low, clear voice. "I was wondering if you want me to finish tilling along the fence or start on the kitchen garden in back? Ginny has been nagging me to plant lettuce. What do you say?"

Thinking it was a rather weak reason for the interruption and wondering how long the hired help had been standing at the front door listening to them, Edna was surprised when Stephen replied in an almost subdued manner. Was his arrogance reserved only for women?

"My wife is the authority when it comes to the grounds." Turning to Peg, he raised an eyebrow. "Margaret?"

When his attention had been momentarily distracted, Edna had caught a motion to her right and flicked her eyes in time to see Peg slip the brooch into a pocket of her slacks. *Out of sight, out of mind*, Edna wondered before she glanced back at the gardener who was also looking at Peg with raised eyebrows.

Impertinent, Edna thought as Peg

responded to the gardener. "That will be fine, Goran. Start on the kitchen garden. The other plots can wait until Virginia's vegetables and herbs are in."

With only a slight nod to acknowledge the order, Goran turned on his heel and headed out the way he'd come. *How the world has changed since Peg's mother's day,* Edna thought, watching the front door close with a loud click. Mrs. Graystocking's gardener would never have entered through the front door and without even knocking.

Stephen's interest returned to his wife. He studied her silently, apparently waiting for her to give him the brooch, although he didn't go so far as to hold out his hand again.

After what seemed an interminable pause, Peg, who had been watching the front door as if wishing it would open again, finally returned his stare. Whatever humor had been left of the morning was gone.

"I am going to keep Mother's pin with me for now, Stephen," she spoke defiantly. "This is not a matter of worth. It's a matter of sentiment. You might not understand, but I wish to have something of Mother's, something personal, that I can touch and look at whenever I feel like it. You have all the other jewelry. I want this."

"You can examine and touch everything we have at the bank, anytime. You know that."

"Visiting possessions in a vault is not the same as having them here at home. Occasionally, I'd like to try something on with an outfit. If it doesn't suit, I'd like the opportunity to pick out something else, without having to traipse to the bank. I don't want to have to remember what was in Mother's or my collection that might go with a particular dress or blouse. I want the option of changing my mind about what I might wear. Why can't you understand that?" Peg's voice broke slightly with her last words.

"You're becoming emotional, Margaret. Pull yourself together. We will discuss this in my office ... privately." This last was spoken with the briefest of glances at Edna.

She was certain Peg did not want to discuss the matter any further, but she heard her say, "I do not want to leave Edna lying alone in our foyer. I'll go ask Virginia to come out here."

"What difference does it make if she lies here alone or not?" He sounded annoyed at the delay.

"The difference is she might have a back spasm, if nothing worse." Peg drew a deep breath before adding more calmly. "If you need to get to the bank, we can discuss Mother's brooch another time."

"Oh, very well. Go get Virginia. I'll be in my office, but I don't have all day, Margaret. I want to settle this before I leave."

He must have turned his back because Edna saw Peg stick out her tongue. They both suppressed laughter as Peg glanced down at Edna and winked before heading off toward the kitchen.

Thank goodness, a spark of humor had returned. *What was it about this morning that sent both of us back to our college days*, Edna wondered. Was it the absurdity of her getting stuck in the fence or was it Stephen's stiff, headmaster attitude that had them feeling like rebellious young girls? Lying on her back in the middle of the Bishops' entryway, she could not decide.

Peg returned a few minutes later with Virginia Hoxie, a large, plain-looking woman who had been working for the Graystockings ever since Edna had known Peg.

"Hello, Virginia," Edna greeted the woman from her position on the floor as if nothing were amiss.

"My goodness, Mrs. Davies." Virginia gaped. "What have you gone and done to yourself?"

"Just a little back strain. I'll be right as rain very soon."

Peg motioned to the chair she had earlier brought from the dining room. "Sit here, Virginia, and entertain Ed while I go speak with Stephen, will you? I shouldn't be long, but if she begins to feel worse in any way, come and get me immediately."

"Right you are, Mrs. Bishop." Virginia lowered her ample body onto the seat, nearly obscuring the chair from Edna's view. "I'll keep a close eye on her. Don't you worry none."

The ensuing silence was broken only by the sound of Stephen's office door closing with a soft snick as the latch fell into place behind Peg.

As if she weren't lying on the floor or

Virginia staring down at her, Edna said, "How are you these days, Virginia. It seems ages since we've had a chance to talk."

"I've been just fine, Mrs. Davies." Peg's housekeeper gently patted the left side of her chest. "Except for watching my old ticker, the doc says I'm fit as a fiddle."

"Oh," Edna was immediately concerned. "Have you been having heart trouble?"

"Nah. Doc says I should take it easy because I had rheumatic fever as a kid, but I'm okay as long as I don't run any marathon races." The plump Virginia chuckled at her own joke.

Searching for a happier topic, Edna said, "How long have you been with Peg?"

The woman smiled, obviously happy to talk about herself. "Fifty-two years, come June," she said with a hint of pride. "My first job after graduating from high school. Mrs. Bishop was two years behind me."

"That would have been the summer she broke her leg." Edna remembered Peg making light of what was probably a painful and boring few months between her sophomore and junior years.

"Ay-yup," Virginia answered, sounding like the old Yankee she was. "I was right there when she had her bicycle accident. Saw the kid who ran her down with his motor bike. He thought he was hot stuff, closing in on a pretty girl riding a two-wheeler, but he startled her so, she steered her bicycle straight off into a ditch. I ran to Miller's store, yelling at them to call an ambulance and the police."

"I didn't know you were the one who saved her life," Edna said, surprised to make the connection with a story Peg had told her years ago. Apparently, she had not only broken her leg, but also had gone into shock from internal injuries caused when she'd been pitched onto the upturned handle bars. Had it not been for her rescuer's quick action, Peg could have died.

"Oh, pshaw," Virginia said, turning pink with pleasure. "I'm sure someone would have come along, if I hadn't been there."

"But didn't you also identify her attacker so the police could arrest him?"

"Well, yes," Virginia admitted, pride winning out over humility.

"So that's when you started working for the Graystockings."

"That's right. I was hired as a sort of personal maid for Mrs. Bishop, or Miss Graystocking, as she was then. I looked after her until she mended and went back to school that fall. Lucky for me, the upstairs maid ran off with her sailor boyfriend about that time, so I took her place. I had no real experience in anything and never had marriage prospects, so I count myself among the fortunate that a job came along when it did."

While Virginia talked, Edna thought that, as many times as Peg or she asked Virginia to use their first names, the woman never dropped the formality of the "Mrs." Now, Edna wondered if it might be because Virginia was in awe of the title, never having assumed it herself. A commotion behind her interrupted Edna's speculations.

Stephen's office door opened abruptly, and his voice echoed around the large, high-ceilinged foyer. "You'll regret it, Margaret."

The words, so tight with emotion, sent a shiver down Edna's spine. What was it besides anger? Fear? Was he that afraid someone would come into the house to steal an old brooch, valuable as it might be? Wouldn't that presuppose word would get around of its existence? *How absurd he's being.* Her concern turned to annoyance that Stephen could take such a pleasurable thing as Peg finding a treasure of her mother's and turn it into a bitter quarrel. *Honestly, the man should be shot*, she thought.

At that moment, Peg stepped into view and spoke softly to Virginia. "Please take this back to the kitchen and don't let Stephen know you have it." Since Peg's back was to Stephen's office, Edna imagined he wouldn't see his wife slip the pin to Virginia or hear the whispered instruction.

Chapter Three

Good old Virginia. As the housekeeper rose, she surreptitiously dropped the brooch into an apron pocket, asking at the same time, "Shall I help you get Mrs. Davies up off the floor, Mrs. Bishop?"

"No. Thank you, Virginia. We can manage." After watching the woman disappear through the dining room and into the kitchen, Peg bent over Edna. "Do you think you're ready to get up?"

Even if her back hadn't been feeling better, Edna would have made a supreme effort to rise. She'd had quite enough of people coming and going and talking above her. She was beginning to feel like a part of the rug.

Taking hold of Peg's hand, she had reached a sitting position when she heard Stephen shut the door to his office, turn a key in the lock and stride heavily across the parquet floor. She caught a quick glimpse of his back as he slammed out the front door without uttering a word. She looked up at her friend. "Very childish behavior," she said, ignoring her own behavior of only moments before. "I don't know how you put up with him. Is he that upset just because you didn't want him to take your Mother's pin to the bank?"

"Oh, he's blown things all out of proportion." Peg replied, helping Edna to stand. The concern on her face belied the lightness of her tone. More seriously, she said, "He had an odd reaction when he saw the brooch, don't you think?" She didn't wait for an answer before adding, "I can't put my finger on just what it was. I felt as though he recognized it, but he couldn't have. It was stolen … lost, I mean, long before we met."

Edna noticed the slip and wasn't about to let her friend glide over it. "You said 'stolen,' Peg, and you yourself have been acting strange since I spotted that darn thing. What is the matter? What's this all about?"

Ignoring her questions, Peg continued with her own string of thoughts, "He's not been himself for several months, but he refuses to talk about it. Keeps denying anything's wrong. Frankly, I'm getting tired of being his punching bag. Figuratively speaking, of course," she amended hurriedly, probably seeing Edna's eyes widen in alarm.

"How are you and Stephen getting on?" The hint of all not being well prompted Edna to pry.

"Some days better than others."

A non-answer, Edna thought. That was true of most relationships. She waited. She knew her friend well enough to realize Peg had more to say and would do so in her own good time.

Peg lifted the chair and returned it to its place near the wall before she turned and spoke. "Sometimes I think I married Stephen because he was so different from Joey." She gave a shaky laugh as tears brimmed in her eyes and threatened to spill down her cheeks. Pulling a tissue from a pocket, she dabbed at her eyes. "Joey was so impetuous, such a spendthrift, I used to worry all the time that we'd lose this house."

"When, in fact, he left you better off than ever," Edna interjected.

"Yes," Peg said, smiling through her tears. "Isn't it ironic? I'd trade all of it to have him back. That stupid accident ..."

Edna thought it best not to dwell on the automobile accident that had claimed Joey's life. She patted her friend's arm. "But we can't see into the future. You had reason to worry when Joey was spending so recklessly. After all, this house has been in your family for five generations and ninety percent of the furnishings have been accumulated by your predecessors."

Peg nodded. "And I do so want to leave it intact for Geoffrey and his children. Since they're expecting their fourth, it looks like the family will go on for a while. It's taking more money than ever to keep this old boat afloat, so I'll want to leave him plenty."

Hoping to keep Peg from getting too maudlin, Edna hurriedly said, "You don't have to worry for a very long time."

"We're getting up there, aren't we." The question was rhetorical.

"Sixty-eight isn't so old," Edna insisted, pretending indignance.

Peg giggled. "Who would have thought a man ten years my junior would have asked me to marry him."

"Well, why not," Edna exclaimed. "You're still a very attractive woman who doesn't look anywhere near her age. Stephen is a lucky man."

It was true. Peg had kept her slender figure and, with the help of her hairdresser, her strawberry-blonde hair which she always wore up in a French twist. Her skin, smooth and nearly unlined, was as free of blemishes as when she was twenty. Edna was sure strangers who saw them together would think her older. She'd let her curls go gray and had to watch her weight regularly, but she didn't resent her friend. They had been too close for too long to hold petty jealousies. These thoughts went fleeting through her mind before she stopped them both from becoming overly sentimental.

"I hadn't planned on this surprise visit, so I've probably upset your morning's schedule. Let me hobble back to the car and get out of your hair."

Peg laughed and protested. "Oh, Ed, since when do you need an invitation to stop by? Next time, though, you might try just walking up to the door and ringing the bell." Brushing her hand lightly over Edna's shoulders to smooth the dress, she went on, "As for my schedule, I have nothing better planned for today than to watch Goran till garden plots. It's probably better that I spend time with you than stand over his shoulder while he churns up the lawn. Joey is probably rolling over in his grave at the destruction of his beautiful grass. Remember how he liked having the entire yard free of obstacles when he had to do the mowing?"

Edna chuckled at a memory of Peg's first husband racing around on his ride-on lawn mower. "He certainly had fun trying to break speed records for cutting the grass."

Smiling ruefully, Peg shoved her hands into the pockets of her khaki slacks. "I miss him, Ed, but not his nerve-wracking pranks or his hair-brained schemes." Shaking her head as if to clear the memory, she voiced the first doubt Edna had heard about the latest project. "I hope all this turmoil will be worth it. The gardens were so beautiful when Mother was alive. I hope I can make them look half as lovely, especially since I'll have to substitute for varieties no longer available."

"I'm sure they'll look wonderful, Peg, and keep an open mind. You don't have to be exact, you know. There are so many new hybrids from which to choose. A mixture of new and old will make it a combination of your garden and your mother's." Feeling better now that she was able to stand upright, Edna stepped over to a wall mirror near the front door and poked a few loose curls into place, preparing to leave.

"Do stay for lunch, Ed. I know you said you were on your way to the Art Club, but the exhibition will be there for another three weeks, and I'd like to show you the design I made for the herb garden from those old photos I found."

Edna turned, tempted by the offer. "I'd love to see your designs and the old pictures. You said your father took them?"

"I think he must have. At least, most of them. They're a bit faded, I'm afraid, which is why I'd like you to look at them, too. I could use a second opinion in identifying some of the plants."

"That sounds like fun, Peg. And lunch sounds good, too, if it won't be any trouble."

"Not at all. You know Virginia. She always cooks too much. Still thinks I need fattening up. I'm sure there'll be plenty for both of us without her having to do a thing but put out an extra plate." Looping her arm through Edna's, she said, "Maybe you could talk with Goran afterwards. Give him some pointers."

Edna chuckled self-consciously at the implied praise. "If he's a professional gardener, I'm sure it's he who could give me some instruction, rather than the other way round. I can hardly be called an expert when I've been working with herbs barely a year." She allowed Peg to pull her toward the kitchen.

"Well, you've got those old journals of Mrs. Rabichek's, not to mention her plants, a shed full of remedies and rafters dripping with bunches of dried stalks."

Peg's words brought images to Edna's mind of the abundant gardens surrounding the house that she and Albert had bought the summer before. The previous owner, having moved to a retirement community near Salem, Massachusetts, to be closer to her children, had left behind several hand-written notebooks and many apothecary bottles, filled and carefully labeled. Full of notes and recipes, the journals had inspired Edna to learn all she could about the plants and shrubs she'd inherited. Already an excellent cook, she was enthusiastically combining her new knowledge with old skills, a hobby that had almost landed her in prison for murder the previous fall. She shuddered at the thought and quickly put it from her mind, as she turned her attention back to the present.

The two women settled themselves at the kitchen table in the solarium extension of the kitchen at the rear of the house, in front of wide windows with a view to the back yard where the Bishop's gardener was busily rototilling patches of earth in an otherwise manicured lawn. As Peg had predicted, Virginia had enough split pea soup to feed half a dozen very hungry people. She served the hearty, homemade soup with squares of hot corn bread and a small lettuce salad before announcing she was off to the grocery store, if they didn't need her for anything else.

Over lunch, Edna and Peg chatted amiably about family and friends and times past. At least Edna felt cheerful, but noticed that Peg, although polite and smiling, had something else on her mind. The two women had met in college, been married within a year of each other and had their first-borns only a week apart. While Edna gave birth to three more children, Peg had raised only the one son. Her Geoffrey and Edna's eldest son Matthew, companions from the crib, were still like brothers. Fortunately, their wives and children all got along well, and the Luccianellos were always invited to the Davies home when the families gathered. Since Peg had married Stephen, she had attended the combined family functions less often and so needed to catch up on family news.

Edna took a last spoonful of Virginia's delicious soup and carefully placed her spoon on the plate beside the bowl. Removing the cozy from the teapot, she refilled first Peg's and then her own teacup with the hot, aromatic orange-pekoe blend. Her curiosity had been aroused and she thought she knew what was occupying her friend's mind. "Okay, Peg, I've done most of the talking so now it's your turn. Tell me about this brooch of your mother's."

When she saw Peg was about to protest, she cut her off quickly. "We know each other too well for you to try and weasel out. I can tell something is bothering you, so you might as well spill it. We've never had secrets from one another, and you'll feel better sharing whatever it is."

Peg sighed and dabbed at the corners of her mouth with a napkin before spreading the linen back in her lap. "You're right, Ed, as usual. I've been going over and over in my mind what could have happened all those years ago. The more I think of it, the worse it becomes. Mother and Father were so unfair to Cherisse."

"Now you really must tell me before I die of curiosity." Edna tried to lighten the gray mood that seemed to have fallen on her friend. "For one thing, who is Cherisse, and for another, how do you know the exact date your mother lost her brooch? It happened so long ago."

"I remember it was the fifteenth of April

because Father was busy with his accountant, getting his taxes finished at the eleventh hour, as usual. Mother wanted him to join us at the Biltmore for lunch and was not happy when he told her he absolutely could not. Father didn't often say no to Mother, so when he did, she'd get into an awful snit."

At the memory, Peg gave a faint smile and shrugged as if to excuse her mother's petulance. "I remember she stormed around the house and then went out to stomp around the gardens. By the time her tantrum was over, she had a large basketful of roses that she brought into the house to arrange and I'm certain Father had been forgiven."

"That's a nice story, Peg, but what does that have to do with the brooch?"

"I'm getting to that." Peg further strained Edna's patience by taking a slow sip of tea before continuing. "When Father came home, he must have thought he had to appease Mother because he told her to get dressed for an evening of dinner and dancing. Of course, she was thrilled and didn't mention that her temper had cooled." Peg smiled with a faraway look in her eyes, apparently amused at her mother's manipulative ways. "She went upstairs to change her clothes and was gone for an unusually long time, even for her. When she finally came down to the living room where Father and I were waiting, she was very upset. She said she wanted to wear her birthday brooch, but couldn't find it. In the long run, she convinced herself it had been stolen."

"And this person Cherisse was accused,"

Edna guessed.

Nodding, Peg looked stricken. "She was Mother's maid. At the time, the only other staff were Virginia and a cook, but neither of them attended to Mother. Cook didn't ever go into the main part of the upstairs. She and Virginia each had her own bedroom and shared a bathroom over the kitchen. Cherisse didn't live in."

"Was anything else missing?"

"No, only the one pin. I helped Mother and Father look for it. We hunted everywhere. Eventually though, Mother confronted Cherisse. When she wouldn't admit to the theft, Mother dismissed her without a reference. Cherisse wasn't able to get a decent paying job after that."

"How do you know? Have you stayed in touch with her?"

"I haven't, but Virginia's remained friends with the family. It was sad, really. Cherisse had two children, a boy and a girl. Guy is two years older than I, and Renee is a year older than Guy. The three of us played together when I was young. I was in my last year of high school and they were both in college at the time this happened. When their mother lost her job, they had to leave school to find work. I haven't spoken to any of the Froissards since Cherisse was dismissed."

"What about her husband? What did he have to say about her dismissal?"

"She was a widow. Her husband was killed in the Second World War. Cherisse brought her children to this country because she had a brother who lived in Providence. He was a bachelor who had died of a heart attack about a year before this all happened. Cherisse never remarried, so it was only the three of them. Of course her children defended Cherisse, said she wouldn't have risked her job and her reputation over something so trivial. Renee and Guy were both very angry with my parents."

"You said Virginia is friends with them, so they must still live in the area."

Peg nodded. "They belong to the same church. Virginia even went to Florida a few years ago with Renee and Cherisse. It was a rare vacation for all of them." Peg was playing with her spoon, rubbing it around on her plate. "I'll ask her how I can contact them." Lifting her eyes to Edna's, Peg almost wailed, "This is terrible, Ed. What will I say to them?"

"You had nothing to do with it. Surely they will understand that." Deciding Peg needed to be distracted, if only until the newness of the discovery wore off a little, Edna said, "You can't do anything until Virginia gets back from shopping, so why don't you show me those pictures of the gardens."

After they'd cleared away the lunch dishes, talk turned to the restoration of the gardens to their early twentieth century condition. Seeming to relax somewhat, Peg brought out and unfolded a sketch she'd made, spreading a number of old photographs over the table so she could explain the design to Edna. They discussed the type and arrangement of the herbs and another half hour vanished quickly while the two old friends put their heads together, comparing the drawing to the pictures.

"You know, I have some of these herbs in my own yard, Peg." Edna said, gathering up the photos. "No sense buying what I can give you. I'll prepare some pots and maybe you can send your gardener down to fetch them."

"That would be wonderful," Peg exclaimed. "Your plants are so healthy. I'll definitely take you up on the offer. I can hardly wait for Goran to start the actual planting. I'm sick of looking at mud."

Edna gazed out the window at the dark-haired young man plodding behind an old red tiller that had obviously seen better days. "I bet you're not tired of looking at the one who's creating all the mud," she remarked, suppressing a laugh as she attempted to recapture the teasing banter of earlier that morning.

Peg's sudden look of astonishment turned to merriment in an instant. "I think you've turned into a dirty old woman, Edna Davies." She giggled mischievously and both women turned back to enjoy the view.

The rain had soaked the soil so that the gardener seemed to strain with the effort of keeping the rototiller moving forward. His heavy boots and the cuffs of his pants were brown with mud. Wagging her eyebrows at Peg, Edna teased, "Where did you find him?"

Peg gently slapped Edna's shoulder. "Well, you old letch, I already told you. Stephen hired him. Goran arrived at the house one morning about three weeks ago and announced that my husband had sent him."

"Nice present," Edna kidded with a wink. Then, more seriously, she added, "I didn't know Stephen had anything to do with the yard or with gardening." She wondered if she might have to adjust her opinion of him after all.

"He hasn't up until now. I was totally surprised when Goran said my husband hired him to help me restore the old gardens, but I'm not one to look a gift horse in the mouth."

"Quite right," Edna said, grinning at Peg. Inwardly, she suppressed an inexplicably uneasy feeling. "What do you supposed possessed him to take such a sudden interest in getting help for you?"

"Probably wants to make sure I keep busy." Peg looked sheepishly at Edna. "I've been bored and restless since he's spending more time at work. When I asked him how he happened to find a gardener, he just shrugged and kissed my cheek. That's his way of avoiding my questions." She paused briefly before adding, "Another reason I was so surprised when Goran showed up was that the restoration was something I had only begun to consider. After finding those old pictures in the hat box, I was mostly thinking out loud when I mentioned to Stephen that it might be nice to have gardens again. It was less than a week later that Goran knocked on the door."

"It is rather odd, but a nice gesture," Edna said, believing only the first part of her statement. Curious about the worker himself, she said, "Let's go talk to him, shall we?" She rose carefully from her chair. Her back had stiffened up with bending over the table, pouring over the old photographs.

As the women approached, Goran was shutting off the machine, apparently finished with the job at hand. Being an amateur portrait artist, Edna attempted mentally to describe the gardener and noted with surprise how very ordinary he looked. Medium height and weight, brown hair and eyes, and no observable scars, moles or blemishes with which to distinguish him from hundreds or thousands of other thirty-something young men.

Having failed to note unusual physical characteristics, she concentrated on his speech and tried unsuccessfully to detect any trace of an accent or grammatical idiosyncrasy that might reveal where he grew up. Nothing. No eastern brogue, no southern drawl or mid-western twang betrayed his origins.

So intent was she on trying to figure the man out, she missed Peg's question. "Sorry, what did you say?" Although speaking to Peg, she was still looking at Goran, so did not miss the fleeting expression before his face relaxed into one of polite attention. Had it been worry? Concern? Certainly it couldn't have been fear. What would he have to fear from them? The impression dissipated like smoke in the wind before she could grab hold of it.

"I was asking if Goran could drive down to your house this afternoon to pick up some of those plants you offered? Will that give you enough time?"

Distracted from her observation of the man, Edna couldn't help smiling at her friend's almost child-like enthusiasm. She had planned on doing some errands before she returned home, but how could she say no? "Of course, this afternoon will be fine. Why don't you come by around four o'clock," she said to Goran.

Soon after, she left to retrieve her car and drive back to South County. During the three quarters of an hour it took her to get home, she thought about the tragic story of the Graystockings' maid and then wondered why Stephen was so adamant about keeping all of Peg's jewelry in his bank vault. Also, why had he taken such an uncharacteristic interest in restoring the gardens, especially to the extent of finding a gardener? Peg always contracted the services needed for the house or the yard, even when she'd been married to Joey. Once, she had told Edna that Stephen seemed impatient with anything that didn't directly relate to his work at the bank. "So, why would he suddenly change his spots?" Edna muttered aloud as she turned onto the crushed-shell driveway that circled around to her front door.

Chapter Four

As Edna turned off the motor and got out of the car, Benjamin came galloping around the corner of the house and jumped onto the hood, purring loudly and lifting his head for her to scratch along his jaw line.

"Hi, Edna. Whatcha doin'?" Mary Osbourne strode through the gap in the stone wall that separated their two properties. Her black Labrador ran beside her, keeping pace with her long-legged stride. Edna rarely appeared in her yard without incurring a visit from her neighbor and Hank who had become her constant companion. Gregarious and not a little eccentric, Mary was a single woman who seemed to know everyone and everything that went on in their small town that was located not far from Rhode Island's resort beaches.

On this sunny April afternoon, for the morning's rain clouds had all but disappeared, she was dressed in jungle camouflage fatigues, one of her preferred costumes. Edna thought her tall, lanky neighbor would blend nicely into the border of laurel bushes that ran along the roadside, if it weren't for her mass of bright red hair. Poor Mary had her cross to bear, trying to tame her natural curls in the climate of southern New England. The morning rain had insured high humidity for the afternoon, and Mary's baseball cap was perched on, rather than containing, her vibrant mane.

She'd been an only child, born when her parents were in their forties and had nearly given up the idea of bearing offspring. She created a drastic change to the Osbournes' life style, and neither they nor the relative they hired as a nanny seemed to know what to do with an energetic, red-headed child.

In her mid-fifties and now alone in the world, Mary lived in the rambling, old family mansion next door to Edna and Albert. Curious and watchful by nature, she kept an eye on the neighborhood from her second story, or even sometimes her third story windows, and listened constantly to the police scanner that had belonged to her father from the days he'd served as a volunteer fireman. Edna frequently noticed curtains flutter in one or another of the Osbourne windows when she and Albert were sitting on their patio enjoying the late-afternoon sun, but she had stopped being the least bit annoyed with her neighbor's intrusiveness since Mary had rescued her from almost certain death the previous fall.

"Where's Al," the neighbor asked now, approaching the car.

"Albert," Edna corrected automatically. "He's off with his pals for a week of golf."

Benjamin bent his head to sniff at Hank who raised his muzzle so the two nearly touched noses. They'd become friends during the several months since Mary had adopted the canine and brought him to live next door. Hank had belonged to Mary's friend Tom Greene who had been Edna's handyman. Once chased and taunted by the dog, Benjamin now took an occasional ride on Hank's back.

"Saw him drive off yesterday afternoon. Didn't see him come home. Just wondered." Mary walked over to stroke Benjamin's back. "So you're bach'n it this week."

"'Til next Sunday. He should be home around lunchtime. Did you need him for something?" Edna hid her smile as she leaned down to rub Hank's ears. She knew darn well Mary was only being nosey.

"Met the new neighbor?" Mary rested a hip against the car and crossed her arms over her chest. Edna thought her neighbor might have been considered plain, but for her lovely green eyes that were definitely the window to her soul. Guileless, Mary would never be able to hide her feelings. At the moment, she was not just a little curious.

"Not yet. The Sharpes must be relieved that someone finally bought their place. I sure am glad it won't be standing empty any longer."

She straightened as she spoke to look across the narrow macadam country lane at the house that was nearly half hidden by the tangle of lilacs and laurels growing in abundance along both sides of the road. The house wouldn't be visible at all except the land sloped upwards and the building sat on top of the hill. A Prudential Gammons Realty sign had decorated the front lawn since the previous autumn when the owners moved out of town. In their hurried departure, they had not waited for the house to sell. Even Allen Gammons, the best realtor in the area, was unable to find a buyer as quickly as the Sharpes had wished. Local gossip and rumor jinxed the place, it seemed, and it was to Gammons' credit that the place was finally off the market.

She turned back to Mary. "Have *you* met them?"

"'S not a 'them'," Mary replied. "New owner's a woman. Been tryin' to meet her, but she doesn't answer the door. Seen her from a distance, is all."

Edna swallowed another smile, knowing it was probably driving Mary crazy to have someone in the area whose acquaintance she hadn't made and whose complete history was unknown to her. Giving Mary a chance to air whatever knowledge she'd gleaned so far, however, Edna asked, "Do you know anything about her?"

"Name's Joanna Cravendorf. I've gone over a few times and knocked on the door, but she doesn't answer. Keeps her curtains drawn, too. Makes me wonder what she's hiding."

"Oh, Mary, you're too suspicious." Edna spoke lightly to take any sting out of her words. "It could be that she's just busy getting settled in and doesn't want to be interrupted."

Mary gave Edna a "get real" look and snorted. "She's been living there for almost three weeks. Should be moved in by now." She frowned when she added, "She does her grocery shopping late at night. Why would she do that if she's not hiding something?"

"I don't know." Edna was growing tired of Mary's skepticism. "Maybe she's allergic to the sun or maybe she's simply a night owl and sleeps during the day. That would also explain why she doesn't answer the door."

Mary shrugged. "Maybe. I guess. But there's something else suspicious about her. I can't find her on the Internet. It's like she doesn't exist."

Edna glanced at her watch and gasped at the time. "I didn't realize it was so late. Sorry, Mary, I'd like to help you figure it out," she said, knowing full well sarcasm would be lost on her neighbor, "but I promised some herbs to a friend. Her gardener will be here to pick them up in less than an hour."

"Need help?"

"Sure, if you have the time. Aren't you working at the hospital today?"

"My volunteer shift got changed. I'm on bookmobile duty and don't have to be there 'til after supper."

Edna led the way along the brick path to the south side of the house. Benjamin jumped off the car and broke into a run while Hank brushed by Edna, trotting to keep up with the cat. Mary brought up the rear.

The side door of the house opened into a large mudroom where Edna kept small gardening tools, bags of potting soil and an assortment of pots, including peat pots for seed starters. Goran would be able to put pots and all into the ground without disturbing the plants' roots again, she decided. By the time she'd grabbed what they'd need and returned outside, Mary was sitting on the weathered wooden bench with her face turned up to the sky, eyes closed.

Just as Edna was thinking she'd lost her helper to the cozy warmth of the late-afternoon sun, Mary's eyes popped open and she smiled. "This was one of my favorite spots when I visited old Mrs. Rabichek. We'd sit here and she'd tell me all about whatever new thing she was going to plant that year."

Old Mrs. Rabichek was "old crazy Mrs. Rabichek," Edna thought, for planting so many poisonous herbs and shrubs on the property. Of course, they could also be used as natural medicines, if one knew how to use them properly, and providing one could determine the strength of whatever it was one was concocting. Potency changes from season to season, depending on rainfall, sunshine and soil conditions. These thoughts brought back unpleasant memories from the previous fall when Edna had been a prime suspect in the death of her handyman, and she quickly dismissed her thoughts with a shudder as she held out a trowel to Mary.

For the next half hour, the two women worked rapidly, filling tiny, organic pots with chive, parsley, dill and a variety of other herbs that had survived the winter beneath a blanket of straw. They were nearly finished and had a row of pots standing on the brick walk that bisected the garden when Edna heard the roar of an engine coming around the driveway. Hurrying to the front of the house, she was in time to watch a black-leather clad man dismount and remove his Darth

Vader headgear. Goran Pittlani balanced the helmet on the seat of his motorcycle before coming forward to greet her.

"Hey, Ms. Davies."

Instead of replying, she continued to stare in astonishment at his mode of transportation. "How are you going to carry my plants back on that thing," she blurted after considering the vehicle for a minute.

When Goran laughed, his eyes twinkled and vertical ridges deepened on either side of his mouth. "The saddlebags hold more than you'd think. I'll manage. Show me what you got."

More than a little doubtful, she motioned with a twist of her head. "This way," she said and led him around the corner to where Mary was swiping dirt off the knees of her pants, having finished pressing the last sprig of lemon thyme into a pot.

Edna introduced them, and the two strangers stood eyeing each other while she studied the collection of newly-filled, little brown pots arrayed along the path. "Shall I put these in paper bags for you," she asked, imagining dirt spilling out into the saddlebags.

"That'd be great." Goran took his eyes from Mary's for the flicker of an instant. "Thanks." His gaze returned to the red-head, who was an inch taller than he, and he smiled.

Amused that Mary seemed to be silently taking Goran's measure as well, Edna went back to the mudroom and returned with a box of brown paper lunch bags. As she approached the pair, she heard Mary ask, "What sort of a name is Goran Pittlani, anyway?"

The man shrugged and, without answering, noticed Edna approaching. With obvious relief, he held out a hand for the bags. "Let me help you."

"Mary and I can do this, but I haven't had time to get the mint. Would you dig some up? It's over there." She motioned toward what looked like a wild, overgrown patch along the stone wall at the back of the yard. "You can use this." She'd made a container out of a slightly larger and heavier paper bag by rolling down a couple of inches at the top.

Grabbing up one of the trowels, Goran strode off to gather mint while Mary placed pots into bags and Edna carried them to the motorcycle. Before long he strode back around the house, reached his bike and, with a swift movement, flipped open one of the leather saddlebags and slipped his package inside. Without a word, he then accepted the small sacks Edna handed to him and stowed them away as well.

When Mary came down the path and handed over the last of the bundles, he picked up his helmet with a flourish. "Thank you, ladies. It's been a pleasure." Donning the headgear and starting the motor, he revved the engine a few times before holding up a gloved hand in farewell as he skidded along the broken shells in the driveway and disappeared onto the road.

As quiet returned to the neighborhood, Mary turned to Edna with a puzzled look on her face. "Didn't you tell me he's your friend's gardener?"

"That's right."

"How come he doesn't know the difference between lemon balm and mint?"

"What do you mean?"

"He had lemon balm in that bag." With those words, Mary gave a sharp whistle. "Oops. I'm late. Gotta go." With that, she spun on her heel and strode across the lawn toward her house. She hadn't gone far when Hank came running across the back yard, tail held high and wagging happily. Lifting a hand in farewell without turning around, Mary called over her shoulder, "Later."

It was typical of her to toss out a verbal grenade and leave before she could be questioned further. Slightly exasperated, Edna shook her head and went to gather up the gardening supplies. Benjamin was waiting for her at the side door.

Chapter Five

After finishing her immediate chores, the most important of which was refreshing her cat's food and water, Edna decided to take a long, hot bath. The morning's strain on her back had been exacerbated by the afternoon's bending and stooping. She'd soak her aching muscles and pour a glass of wine before deciding what to make for supper. On second thought, she poured the wine first and took the glass upstairs.

She'd just lowered herself into the warm, lavender bubbles of her bath, had leaned back and closed her eyes when she heard the phone ringing in the bedroom.

"Drat."

Keeping her eyes shut, she told herself that the answering machine would pick up if the caller really wanted to leave a message. She let the hot water sooth her muscles until it began to cool. Finally, reluctantly, she stepped from the tub, toweled dry and slipped into a dark blue, velour robe. One of her pleasures when Albert was out of town was to put on something really comfortable—sweats were another favorite—and peruse the refrigerator and pantry for a pickup supper. This evening, she made a Greek salad with her favorite lemon and olive oil dressing. Along with garlic, she chopped and added fresh oregano leaves to the dressing from a pot on the window sill above the sink.

Taking salad and wine into the small office across the front hall from the kitchen, she sat at her desk to eat while she listened to the day's phone messages and checked her e-mail. Benjamin, savvy to her habits, was already curled into a ball on the cushion of the guest chair beside the desk. As she had thought, the call coming in when she'd been in the bathtub was from Albert.

"Hi, sweetheart. We had a good day today. Weather's a little cool, but great for being out on the course. I'm about to join the boys for dinner, so I'll call you when we get back to the condo."

Edna almost laughed aloud. If her husband had shot more than a mediocre golf game, he would have told her his score, bragging a little. *Well*, she thought, taking a bite of salad, *this is only their first full day at the resort village. I'll hear about the good shots in another day or two.*

After eating, washing her dishes and cleaning the kitchen, she went into the living room to sit in her favorite wing-back chair, don the half glasses she wore for close work, and pick up her knitting. She was listening to an audio recording of "Middlemarch" by George Eliot and counting stitches in the tiny, forest-green sweater she was making for her newest grandson when the doorbell rang.

The clock on the CD player at her elbow read 7:43.

"Who in the world …" she pushed herself from the chair, frowning, and leaving her muttered sentence unfinished.

Before opening the door, she turned on the

porch light and looked through the fisheye lens to see a young woman staring steadily back at her, obviously aware that she was being observed. She clutched a large manila envelope against her middle. Frowning with curiosity, Edna opened the door.

"I am *so* sorry to bother you," the young stranger began immediately, "but may I come in for a minute?" Stepping across the threshold without waiting for an answer, she said, "My name is Jaycee Watkins. I just moved in across the street."

Watkins? Although she couldn't recall the name Mary had mentioned that afternoon, Edna was certain it hadn't been Watkins. *Perhaps a married name?* She figured the woman to be in her early thirties. Medium-brown hair was plaited into a single braid which hung a few inches below the nape of her neck. A few stray tendrils curled at her temples. Dark circles beneath her large, brown eyes were the only stains in an otherwise confident appearance. She stood in the hall, looking pleasant but unsmiling.

When Edna closed the door against the evening's chill, her young visitor seemed to loosen her grip on the envelope. "I wonder if you would help me?" She spoke the request both as a question and an appeal.

Edna felt herself stiffen. Was Jaycee in some sort of trouble? She wasn't acting particularly nervous, but she did seem tense. Without voicing her concerns, Edna simply introduced herself and said noncommittally,

"What do you need?"

Jaycee held up the envelope before pulling it back to her chest, seeming reluctant to part with it just yet. "Would you hang onto this for me?"

Edna didn't know what to say. It seemed like an innocent request, if somewhat unusual.

Jaycee rushed on before the silence could grow. "They're some papers that I don't want to keep in my house … in case of fire or something, you know. I haven't decided what bank I want to use in town, but as soon as I do, I'll put them in a safe deposit box."

"Why me?"

The question brought a tentative smile to the young woman's lips and a slight flush of embarrassment to her cheeks. "I've been watching the neighborhood since I moved in a few weeks ago, and I've noticed that most everyone is gone during the day. There's one woman who's knocked on my door a few times. I know she probably just wants to be friendly, but she seems …" Jaycee hesitated, her flush deepening before she finished lamely, "a little odd."

Edna coughed to hide a laugh. "You must mean Mary. She *is* a bit eccentric, but very good-hearted. She'll drive you to distraction asking personal questions, but she means well."

"You and your husband seem like nice people, and there's usually lots of activity at this house." She furrowed her brow. "I think if anything were to happen, like a fire or something, someone would be around to sound an alarm. I wouldn't worry about my papers if you could keep them here for a few days."

"Well, I guess I could ..." Edna began slowly, still hesitant, but she wasn't allowed to finish.

"Thank you so much." Sounding as if a great weight had been lifted from her shoulders, Jaycee pushed the envelope into Edna's hands. "I promise I'll be back soon and we can talk. Get to know each other. You know." Sidling to the door as she spoke, she opened it and slipped out into the night, repeating, "Thank you so much," before she disappeared into the night.

Closing the door, Edna stared unseeing for several heartbeats, trying to straighten out in her mind what had just occurred. Shaking her head, she finally examined the manila envelope. An inch or two of clear, heavy package tape had been smoothed over the clasp that held the flap down. The envelope was not overly bulky and felt to Edna as if it contained a thickness of standard-sized paper. Written in a neat cursive on the front were the words, "Property of J.W. If not collected in person, please phone ..."

Reading the number, she recognized the area code for Chicago. She knew the code because Chicago was where her sister lived. Edna shrugged, realizing she'd have to wait for another visit from Jaycee to find answers to the questions going around in her head. Stepping into her office, she slipped the envelope into a desk drawer before returning to the living room.

No sooner had she figured out where she was in the little sweater pattern and begun to knit again when she heard the front door open. *Did I forget to lock it?* Her heart began to thump in double-time before her daughter's voice rang out. "Hello. It's me."

"I'm in the living room, dear." Edna called back, as her heart rate returned to normal.

The youngest of her four children strode into view and threw herself onto the sofa, facing Edna with a look of utter dejection.

Deciding to ignore what she knew from experience was her child's self-pitying attitude, Edna said, "You're looking particularly lovely this evening. What are you doing here—and all dressed up on a Monday night?"

Starling lived in the Back Bay area of Boston where she was co-owner of a photography studio. She was tall and willowy, having her father's physique. Instead of his pale blondeness, however, she had her mother's auburn coloring. Typically, she wore slacks and a pullover, but this evening, she had on a black, sleeveless, fitted sheath dress with a V-shaped neckline. Her straight, shoulder-length hair had been pulled back and pinned at the crown. A slender, onyx pendant that matched her earrings hung from a thin silver chain around her neck.

"I *thought* I was going to have dinner with Charlie, but he's working … *again.*
Why did you ever fix me up with a cop?"

Edna lowered her knitting and looked over the top of her glasses. "As I remember it, dear child of mine, you asked me if he were married, and he asked me if I'd mind him calling you. I said 'no' to you both."

Starling paused and frowned for a few seconds before bursting into laughter. "Got me there, Mommy Dearest. Your defense is indisputable." She laughed again as Edna, smiling, resumed her knitting.

"But it's so frustrating," Starling wailed. "He said he'd have the next few evenings free, so I decided to bring my cameras and shoot around South County for a couple of days. We were supposed to meet at that new restaurant in Narragansett. I was even on time, but just as I was pulling into the parking lot, he called and said he couldn't make it." She turned and fell dramatically sideways to press her face into a sofa pillow, muffling a melodramatic scream of disappointment. Coming up for air, she groaned, "He was assigned to a new case late this afternoon and told to get on it *yesterday*."

During her daughter's tirade, Edna had turned off the CD player, and now she gave up trying to count stitches. Removing her eyeglasses and setting them on the side table next to the player, she said in what she hoped was a sympathetic tone. "Surely, you'll be able to see him tonight. He has to eat sometime."

"You'd think so, wouldn't you?" Starling pouted and clutched the pillow to her chest with both arms.

"Don't sulk, dear, it's unbecoming, and your face will freeze like that." Edna teased with a quote from her own grandmother who used to drive everyone to distraction with her commonplace advice.

As she'd hoped, her child chuckled and regained her more-typical sunny disposition. Edna knew this daughter's peevishness was mainly for immediate dramatic effect and not deep-seated petulance as would be the case with Diane, child number two.

Of Edna's four children, Starling was the only one who hadn't yet married. She'd had a number of suitable boyfriends over the years, but at age thirty-two, she hadn't yet found someone she couldn't live without. Edna thought maybe her current interest, Charlie Rogers, might be different. For one thing, he wasn't forever at her beck and call.

"Maybe if I commit a crime ..."

Edna's ruminations were shattered by Starling's words. She feigned a look of shock. "But he's a *homicide* detective."

The comic look of horror that followed her words brought forth Starling's trilling laughter again before she sobered.

"Don't remind me. He wouldn't be half so busy if he weren't always volunteering to work with other police departments. His own work should be enough."

"Oh?" Edna's curiosity was piqued. "Is he on loan again?"

"Beats me. He never talks about what he's doing. Now I know how it must have felt being married to Dad—you know, patient confidentiality and all."

"Charlie is claiming 'patient

confidentiality'?" Edna purposely misunderstood.

Starling squinted at her, probably trying to figure out if Edna were kidding, then gave her a weak smile. "Of course not. Whenever I ask him about his work, he doesn't *say* anything—just looks at me with those baby blues, or baby hazels, and raises his eyebrows. It's aggravating."

Realizing her daughter was in no mood for further teasing, Edna tried changing the subject. "Did you know we have a new neighbor?"

At that moment, the doorbell rang. Noticing from the mantelpiece clock that it was nearly nine, she almost smiled at Jaycee's observation of the "daily activity" at this house and then wondered who would be showing up at this hour without phoning first.

"I'll get it." Starling jumped up with excessive, nervous energy and headed for the front hall, returning moments later smiling up at and holding onto the arm of police Detective Rogers.

"Hello, Charlie," Edna said with surprise. "I thought you were working. Have you come to steal my girl away?"

"She *is* quite a girl, isn't she," Charlie said, admiring the view as Starling moved in front of him to settle again on the couch. Sitting beside her, he turned to Edna. "Can't stay long, but I was in the neighborhood and thought I'd stop by to see what you ladies were up to."

Edna suspected Charlie hadn't just happened to be in the neighborhood—and how did he know Starling hadn't driven back to Boston? He was the one who was up to something. She studied him as he made idle chit-chat for several minutes. That wasn't like him either. When Charlie was on duty, he was totally dedicated to his cases and didn't spend time socializing or spouting pleasantries. Five minutes after he'd arrived, the detective stood.

"Better get back to work or the chief will have my badge."

When the two young people had gone-- Starling walking Charlie to the door--Edna picked up her knitting again. Before starting to count stitches, she muttered softly to the empty room, "Now I wonder what that was all about?"

Chapter Six

Early the next morning, Edna found herself alone for breakfast, except for Benjamin who sauntered out of the mudroom where he slept in a fleece-lined bed most nights. Finishing a bowl of cereal with banana slices, she poured a second cup of coffee and folded the newspaper to the puzzle section. She picked up a pencil to begin the crossword and wondered why Albert hadn't phoned back last night. It wasn't like him.

As the thought came to her, the phone rang, so of course she thought it must be Albert. Now that her husband was retired from his medical practice, the caller wouldn't be someone from the hospital or a patient seeking medical advice before Albert left for the clinic. These days, only family called before eight in the morning. Instead of going across the hall to her small office to check the caller's id, she reached for the kitchen receiver hanging on the wall near the end of the table.

"Good morning, dear."

Three long seconds of silence followed before a male voice said hesitantly, "Good morning."

Edna stifled a laugh. "That you, Charlie? Sorry. I was expecting Albert to phone. If you're calling for Starling, she drove home last night after you left."

"I know. Actually, I want to talk to you

and figured I'd catch you before you started your day. Mind if I stop by the house?"

"I always have time for my favorite peace officer." She wondered if he sensed her broad smile.

"Thanks. I'll be right over."

"I'll make fresh coffee."

Edna had met Charlie Rogers the previous fall when a friend's house had been robbed of valuable antiques. Charlie was the detective assigned to the case. Shortly thereafter, Edna had been a suspect in the death of her handyman, another incident that put her in almost daily contact with Charlie. Through the challenge of proving her innocence, she and the detective had developed a mutual liking and respect. She was pleased when he began to date her daughter.

Almost as soon as the receiver was back in the cradle, the phone rang again, ending her ruminations. She was certain this time it was Albert. "Good morning, dear."

"Hello, sweetie," came a female voice.

Edna refused to laugh. She bit the inside of her cheek to stop a fit of giggles before answering. "How are you this morning, Peg?"

"Much better after such a warm greeting, Ed. And you?"

"Feeling fine, thanks. To what do I owe the honor of this early call?"

"Just something I was wondering about and decided to check with you before I started work in the garden."

"Oh?"

"I thought we had agreed to plant mint next to the tool shed."

"That's right. Mint by the shed."

"Then where is it, and what am I supposed to do with the lemon balm he brought back? I don't remember discussing it as part of the gardens."

The question brought Goran Pittlani to Edna's mind. "I was going to call you this morning about that very thing, Peg. I still want to visit the RISD exhibition at the Art Club, so I thought I'd drive up to Providence again today. I'll bring you some mint, and we need to talk about your gardener."

"My gardener?" Peg was obviously mystified.

"Yes, your gardener. I can't talk now. I'm expecting Charlie at any minute, and I'm also hoping for a call from Albert. I'll see you later and explain."

"You've certainly aroused my curiosity, Ed. I'm glad you're coming back into town, because I have something else to discuss with you. Remember my telling you about Mother's maid whom she accused of stealing her brooch?"

"Yes."

"Well, I've learned from Virginia that Cherisse is still living. She's in a nursing home. I don't know if she'll want to see me, but I ought to let her know we found the brooch. I *must* apologize to her, Ed. I have no idea how I'll make it up to her for all those years of disgrace caused by my family. You can call me a coward, but I need you to come with me to see her. Can you fit that into your schedule this afternoon?"

Besides sensing a touch of insecurity, unusual for her friend, Edna wondered if she also heard a bit of loneliness in Peg's voice. After a brief pause during which she mentally arranged her schedule for the day, she said, "Of course I'll go with you. Shall I pick you up after lunch?"

"I need to get out of the house. Why don't I meet you at the Art Club? A walk in the fresh air will do me good, and we can go to lunch somewhere afterwards."

"Sounds good to me. I'll be there at noon when they open." Before she could say more, the doorbell rang. "Gotta go, Peg."

Hastily replacing the receiver, she stood and turned toward the hall just as the phone rang again. Reaching back around to the wall phone, she wanted to say "Davies Madhouse" but said instead, "Davies residence. Please hold." Without waiting for a response, she put down the receiver and hurried to the front door where, standing on the stoop, Charlie was silhouetted in the morning sunshine.

"Come in. I'm on the phone." She greeted him and, at the same time, turned and raced back to the kitchen.

She was so harried, she lost her manners. "Who's this?"

"Edna? It's me. What's going on?" This time it was Albert.

Wouldn't you know, she thought with a wry smile. Aloud, she said, "The phone's been ringing non-stop this morning, or so it seems. Charlie's just stopped by, and I was about to make a fresh pot of coffee. What's happening at your end? I thought you were going to call back last night."

"Didn't have a chance. Stan's had a heart attack. I was in the emergency room all night, sitting with him and conferring with his doctors. I'm at the condo now, about to catch a few hours' sleep before going back to the hospital."

Edna felt the shock of the news course through her body and chill the pit of her stomach. "Oh, no. Is he okay? I mean …" *Of course he's not okay*, her mind's logic kicked in.

"He's alive. They admitted him to ICU early this morning. He's being closely monitored and will undergo some tests today to determine how much damage has been done to his heart."

"When did it happen?"

"Last night at the restaurant. Middle of dinner. Luckily, the maitre d' was on the ball and dialed nine-one-one immediately."

"Have you talked to Bea?" Edna thought of the shock Stan's wife must be feeling and made a mental note to call her.

"I just got off the phone with her a few minutes ago. She's flying out this afternoon. Look, sweetheart, I only called to let you know what's going on, but I'm dead on my feet. I need to get some sleep and get back to the hospital."

"Okay, dear. Keep me posted and, when you can, let me know what your schedule will be. I assume you'll stay there until Stan is out of danger, at least."

"That's my plan for the moment. We've got the condo for the week and, since it's only Tuesday, we'll keep things as they are for now. Bea will stay here in Stan's room."

"Let me know if there's anything I can do. And take care of yourself. I don't want *you* ending up in the hospital."

Typically, he hung up without another word.

"What's wrong?" Charlie straightened from where he had been leaning against the kitchen sink. "Who's in the hospital?"

"One of Albert's golfing buddies," She wandered over to the counter, still feeling dazed and numb with the news. Briefly, she related the conversation, then added some background for his benefit. "Stan and Albert have been friends ever since they were thrown together as roommates their freshman year in college."

"Where was that?" Charlie seemed to be making conversation to ease her mind from the current crisis.

"Over here, in Kingston."

The University of Rhode Island was less than ten miles from the home Edna and Albert had bought the previous summer. When he retired from his medical practice, he'd wanted to move where he wouldn't always be running into his old patients. A clean break was good for him and good for the woman who'd taken his place at the clinic. He didn't feel comfortable second-guessing her diagnosis when someone would stop him on the street and ask his opinion.

"Stan and his wife moved to Cranston a few years after Albert and I bought our house in Providence, so we've all been close for years. In fact, Stan and Bea have been talking recently of moving down here to the southern shores when he retires."

"Oh?" Charlie sounded as if he were fascinated with this family history. Edna couldn't help smiling at him as he reached for a banana-nut muffin she'd put on a plate near him. He broke a piece off of one and popped it into his mouth as she continued with her story.

"I'm afraid Albert won't have much of a golf-getaway now. He'll spend his time between meeting with Stan's doctors and assuring Bea that everything is going to be fine. A patient's health and well-being has always come first with my husband. That's one of the traits that made him such a good doctor." *And one reason I fell in love with him nearly fifty years ago*, she thought with some inner pride but did not say aloud. Charlie was beginning to feel like another son to her, but she didn't typically wear her heart on her sleeve.

As she spoke, she spooned fresh grounds into a clean coffee filter. Charlie rinsed the pot and filled the coffee maker's reservoir with cold water. She added apple slices to the plate of muffins, guessing that Charlie hadn't made himself a decent breakfast.

"Well, nothing I can do for Stan or Bea at the moment," she said, finally throwing off the doldrums. "What brings you out here so early, especially since Starling went back to Boston." A thought stuck her then. "Did you think she'd gone right back home after you had to cancel your dinner plans? Were you surprised to see her here when you dropped by last night?"

"As a matter of fact ..." Charlie gave her one of his disarmingly boyish grins. "It *was* you I came by to see. Didn't want to say anything in front of Starling, though. Might've upset her to hear she wasn't first on my mind."

"I see," she said, although she really didn't. She plucked two mugs off a wooden rack and filled them with coffee. Handing one to Charlie and picking up the muffin plate, she motioned for him to sit at the table. Once they were settled, she prompted, "Okay. You've got my attention. If *she* isn't the first thing on your mind ..." at this she smiled, "what have you come to see *me* about?"

At that, he became his professional self. "Your new neighbor," he replied. Helping himself to another muffin, he took a bite, chewed, swallowed and sipped some coffee.

"What about her?"

"Have you met her?"

"Yes, as a matter of fact, she knocked on my door and introduced herself just last night." Edna wondered if she should tell him about the envelope. Jaycee hadn't said it was top secret nor had she asked Edna not to tell anyone about it, but her instinct told her to wait and first hear what Charlie had to say. She raised the mug to her lips, waiting for him to lead the conversation. His next question wasn't one she expected.

"You're good at observing people. Would you describe her for me?"

Slowing lowering the mug, she stared at him across the table. He stared back. Nothing in his expression gave away what he might be thinking. "What's this about, Charlie?"

"Might be nothing. Before I say anything, I'd like to know if she's the person I think she is. Tell me what she looks like."

Edna gathered her thoughts and began to speak slowly. "I'd say she's about Starling's age. Not as tall. More my height. I'd say maybe five five or five six, a hundred ten pounds, give or take. Brown hair, fairly nondescript. She was wearing it in a braid last night, but I'd say it's a few inches past her shoulders. I wouldn't say she's a beauty, but she's pretty enough with big, brown eyes and a few freckles on her nose. Is that the sort of description you're looking for?"

"It'll do." He took a slow drink while Edna watched him curiously.

"Can you tell me what this is about?" She knew from working with him in the past that he wasn't always free to explain details concerning an on-going case.

"Will you keep this between us for the time being?"

Her curiosity cranked up another notch. "Of course. I won't say a word."

"I got a call yesterday from a friend in Chicago. Well, he's not a close friend. I know Dietz from when we worked on a national, organized-crime task force a few years back."

She thought of the phone number she'd seen on Jaycee's envelope, remembering the Chicago area code. He had her attention now, and she waited for him to continue.

"He asked me to check on a woman who recently moved into this neighborhood. Dietz said he wasn't sure what name she was using, but I couldn't get him to explain what he meant by that. Being the detective that I am," at this, he grinned, his hazel eyes twinkling, "I looked up recent sales in town. Surprised the heck out of me when I learned the only home bought by a woman was right across the street from you. I checked with Allen Gammons at the realty company that handled the sale. He told me the place sold to a Joanna Cravendorf, but he never met the woman. Apparently, she's elderly, lives in Florida. Gammons said the closing was handled by her lawyer."

Edna shook her head, furrowing her brow. "When my neighbor came by last night, she introduced herself as Jaycee Watkins and she's definitely not elderly. I'd say she's in her early thirties, certainly no older. Are you certain about the information you got from Mr. Gammons?" Edna remembered how her visitor had pronounced the name 'JAYcee' with the emphasis on Jay. "Could she be Joanna Cravendorf and her name is simply a fusion of her initials? Maybe Watkins is a married name."

Charlie raked both hands through his thick brown hair. It didn't look very different from when he'd arrived on her doorstep, and Edna wondered, amused, if this were how he normally combed his hair.

"Dietz was in a hurry when he called. Said he didn't have time to answer questions, but he'd explain when he could." Charlie stood and began to pace the length of the kitchen, as if motion helped him to think. Settling back in her chair, she watched him and waited.

"About all he said was that a friend had recently moved to this area and would I keep an eye on her. Nothing official, nothing obvious. He said he didn't want to draw attention to her, but said he gave her my cell number, just in case she needed to get in touch with someone locally. That was all. Said he had to go, he'd call me and explain later, and he hung up."

"Why not go across the street, knock on her door and introduce yourself? You could ask her how she knows your friend Dietz."

"That certainly would be the easy way." Charlie smiled at her before continuing, "But my gut feeling is to find out more about her before I do that."

She nodded, realizing she had the same instinct when it came to revealing the envelope to him, first find out more about Jaycee. "Do you think Jaycee Watkins is the one you're looking for? Maybe she isn't if the homeowner is an elderly woman."

"From your description, I'd say she's the one."

"Does Dietz have a photo of her he can

send? That would be the best way to make certain you have the right person. Even if you were to meet her face-to-face, without a picture you can't be sure."

Charlie paused in his pacing to study her as he thought about it. "He didn't mention a picture, and I didn't have time to ask."

"I might be able to sketch a fairly accurate portrait from memory. You could send it to him to verify she's the one he's asking about."

Charlie's face brightened. "Good idea. That'll help."

"I don't have time this morning. Maybe this afternoon. In the meantime, if we assume the woman across the street is the person he's looking for, why does he want you to watch her?"

"Not 'watch her' so much as 'keep an eye out for her.' You know, to make sure she's all right. He said it was nothing official, just a personal favor."

"But he didn't tell you *why*?"

"No. He was in a hurry. Said he couldn't talk, but would call later."

"Could she be an old girlfriend of his? What if this is some sort of long-distance stalking he's having you do?"

"Nah." Charlie snorted a laugh. "Dietz is happily married with two kids and another on the way. I think, even if he wanted to, he doesn't have time to cheat on his wife."

"Fair enough. So, what do you want me to do?"

"Since you live so close, I thought maybe

you could get to know her and be my eyes and ears until I find out a little more about her and the woman who bought the house."

"I'll do what I can, of course, but I'm *not* going to act like Mary." She smiled at the image she'd invoked of herself wearing the latest camo-fatigues, hiding in the bushes on the fringes of Jaycee's property, binoculars to the ready. Charlie laughed, probably having conjured up a similar vision.

"Seriously," she went on, "I will not spy on the poor girl. I'll be as attentive a neighbor as I can be without intruding on her privacy. And you should call this Dietz person back and get more information. I don't know about you, Charlie, but I smell something fishy."

Chapter Seven

After arranging to contact Charlie when she returned from Providence later that day, Edna spent some time in her herb garden. It was a perfect spring morning as far as she was concerned, sunny with a touch of coolness to the air that made it pleasant to work outside. She had orange, caraway and wild thymes she wanted to plant, in addition to the regular garden and lemon thymes already growing among the rocks.

Over the winter, she had read that thyme, a member of the mint family, is attractive to bees and repulses other insects. *I'm all for that*, she thought, setting down the small pots. She thought she might try making aromatic sachets of the herb to put in her linen cupboard, as they had in the old days.

She dug three small holes with her trowel, each in a different area of the garden. Finishing the last, she stood up and looked back at her work, only to spot Benjamin scraping more dirt out of the first hole before going to the second to make that one a little deeper. Very seriously, he moved to the hole at her feet to do the same before leaping onto the nearby brick path and settling down to groom the soil out of his paws. Highly entertained by her cat, Edna wished she had a camera handy.

"Thanks, my friend," she said with a chuckle. Watching the time, she finished up in the herb garden, dug up a few mint plants for Peg, and headed indoors to shower and change her clothes.

An hour later, she paused at the end of her driveway to study the house across the street for a minute, before pulling out onto the road. As she picked up Route 1 and headed for the city, she thought about Jaycee's face with the idea of making the sketch for Charlie. She puzzled over what the young woman's story might be and why someone from the Chicago police might want to have her watched. Personal or business, she wondered. Traffic began to pick up as she merged onto Interstate 95. Forgetting about her neighbor for the time being, she focused on her driving and watched for the exit to Memorial Boulevard.

When she reached the historic clubhouse, she parked in the lot off Benefit Street and walked around to the front entrance. Formed in 1880 to encourage an appreciation of art in the community, the Providence Art Club was one of the oldest art clubs in the country. The house, originally the residence of Obadiah Brown, was built in 1790. Club founders took it over in 1887, creating studios and galleries and providing a gathering place for members. Club membership was restricted and included both artist and non-artist categories. Edna had been an artist member for eight years and had even won a few awards for her portraits. She preferred to paint in oils, but occasionally someone's face would prompt her to sketch in pen and ink.

The exhibition in the Maxwell Mays Gallery was for the graduating seniors from the nearby Rhode Island School of Design, or "RIZ-dee" as it was commonly called. RISD, consistently the highest ranked fine arts college in the country, was contiguous to Brown University on College Hill and only a short walk from the Art Club. Edna made it a point to visit student exhibitions each spring, interested to observe trends from one graduating class to the next.

"I like that one particularly, don't you?" Peg had come up quietly and stood looking over Edna's left shoulder at an Impressionistic-style oil painting of a walled garden containing a profusion of flowers in bright yellows, reds, purples, greens and oranges.

"Yeeessss," Edna drew out the word, thoughtfully, tilting her head slightly as she studied the work. Straightening to turn to her friend, she nodded to more artwork on an adjacent wall. "There are so many talented young artists in this room. I'm almost overwhelmed."

Peg smiled and hooked her arm through Edna's. "Then let's get out of here and go have lunch. Are you ready?" Her smile faded and she looked momentarily apologetic. "I'm not rushing you, am I? I purposely took a long walk to give you time to enjoy yourself. I spent an afternoon here last week, so I knew you'd like it."

"What did Stephen think of it?" Edna assumed Peg had attended with her husband.

"He hasn't seen it yet. Lately, it seems he hasn't much time for anything except his dusty old bank."

Peg's tone was light, but Edna detected a

sadness in her words. When she looked at her friend, however, Peg's expression was cheerful, as if she were determined to push negative thoughts away. "Come on. Let's go over to the Capital Grille. I'm dying for some lobster bisque."

Edna had to laugh at her friend's enthusiasm, feigned or not. "It's really the sherry they drizzle on it that you like. Admit it."

"Never," Peg said, her eyes shining. "The way you talk, people will think I'm nothing but an old lush."

Even after one o'clock on a Tuesday afternoon, there was a good crowd at the Grille, but the women were seated almost immediately in the lounge area. It was cozily warm in the room and smelled faintly of cooking spices.

Peg was wearing a blue-gray jacket dress that complemented the color of her eyes. Once the waiter retreated with their orders for white wine and bowls of lobster bisque, she slipped off the jacket and draped it over her chair back.

Edna nodded at the sparkling pin on her dress. "Did you fix the clasp?"

"I bent it a little so it would hold, but I do need to take it to a regular jeweler to look at."

"So Stephen hasn't yet squirreled it away in the depths of his bank vault."

Peg tucked her chin to look down at the brooch. "No, but I have to hide it from him. I'm sure he'd grab it, if I'd left it out on my dressing table." She wrinkled her nose at Edna. "Let's talk about something else."

"Fine with me." Edna picked up her linen

napkin, focusing her attention for a moment on opening it and laying the silky smoothness over her lap before asking, "What are you going to say to Cherisse? Have you thought about it?"

Before Peg could reply, the waiter returned. She waited in silence as he carefully served them wine and water. He'd added a thin wedge of lemon to each water glass. When he was again out of earshot, Peg sighed heavily.

"I haven't thought of much else since I learned Cherisse was still living. I had the impression she was on her way out when they returned from Florida three years ago. How do I tell her about Mother's pin turning up, after all these years?"

"Literally turning up," Edna said dryly, showing only a hint of amusement in her expression, but hoping to lighten Peg's mood.

"Yes," her friend replied with equally feigned solemnity, but her eyes regained some sparkle. She held her glass up in a silent acknowledgement of the pun before lowing it to take a sip. It was only after this small bit of drama that she looked at Edna more seriously. "I really *have* been thinking of what to say and I'm still not certain how to begin. I feel terrible for the poor woman, but fifty years have passed. Do you think I'm being wise to rake it all up again?"

Edna tasted her Chardonnay before speaking. "Virginia knows the pin has been found, doesn't she?"

"Yes."

"And she's remained friends with Cherisse

and the family?"

"Yes." Peg gave another sigh. "I see what you mean, and yes, I'd rather confess to them myself. Even if Virginia hasn't already said something to them, I'd rather they hear an apology from me before any more time goes by."

"Do you think Virginia *wouldn't* mention it?"

"She might not. Out of loyalty to me, I suppose."

"Have you asked her?"

"No. We haven't talked about it specifically. I think she's been waiting for me to bring up the subject. I haven't wanted to talk about it until I get it all sorted out in my head. Do you know what I mean?"

"Yes, I think I do. Do you want to practice your approach before we leave for the nursing home?"

"I don't think so, but thanks for the offer. I have so many different thoughts spinning around in my head, I'll probably wait to see how the conversation goes once we get there. It may all depend on how frail or how alert Cherisse is. According to Virginia, she's been declining fairly rapidly lately, but mostly physically, not mentally. If her mind isn't wandering and if she remembers who I am, I think I'll begin by saying I wanted to visit her and break the silence that has existed for so many years. I'll say that Virginia told me only recently about Cherisse's failing health. What do you think?"

"Sounds like a good way to start," Edna

agreed. "Will you wear the pin when you speak to her?"

"That would be rubbing it in, don't you think?" Peg frowned at Edna. "You know I have better manners than that."

"Just checking, since you're wearing it at the moment."

"I brought a little box to put it in until …" Peg hesitated before continuing, "or *if*, I decide to show it to her. As I said, it all depends on her condition and what sort of reception I get."

Edna noticed the waiter approaching and reached for her wine glass in a silent gesture to Peg that they were about to be interrupted. Large, shallow bowls of hot, pink and cream soup were placed before them and after a brief conversation with the waiter that "no, they were fine for now and didn't need anything further at the moment," the two women were alone again. Neither spoke until they had tasted the bisque. Both agreed it lived up to and probably exceeded their expectations.

"I wonder how freshly chopped basil would taste on this," Peg said.

"Thyme is more common in lobster dishes." Edna took a small spoonful and rolled it around on her tongue, trying to imagine it with basil. "Hmmm. I think the jury will remain out on your suggestion. I'll try it next time I have lobster. I might also try rosemary or even a bit of lemon grass."

"Better yet, try it with hot rosemary bread, right out of the oven." Peg's eyes glowed with the thought she'd conjured up.

"Speaking of herbs," Edna hesitated for a second or two as she put her spoon down. "What do you know about your gardener?"

"Goran? What should I know?" The edges of Peg's mouth began to lift. "He's good at plowing up the lawn. He digs holes and puts plants where I tell him to. And, as you so lasciviously pointed out yesterday, he looks good doing it."

Edna couldn't help laughing, but then became serious. "But what do you really know about him? Where does he come from, and what made him decide to take up gardening? What sort of gardener doesn't know the difference between mint and lemon balm?"

"I assume Stephen checked his references." Peg looked down at the brooch as she unpinned it from her dress, avoiding Edna's eyes.

"That's another thing," Edna said, not able to keep the annoyance from her voice. "Why did Stephen hire him when he's never done anything like that before? Does he even know how to conduct an interview for household help?"

At that, Peg did look up at Edna, a smile playing around her lips. "Just because Goran doesn't know everything there is to know about gardening, doesn't make him an evil man." Suddenly, she couldn't contain a chuckle. "Besides, he's promised to give me a ride on his bike. I can't fire him until I have my first motorcycle ride, can I?"

Edna gave a short laugh. "I give up." *For now*, she thought.

Peg removed a small jeweler's box from her handbag, carefully wrapped the brooch in a bit of tissue paper and placed it on the cotton in the box. Replacing the tiny lid, she put the box back into her bag. Her smile had faded as she'd concentrated on this chore. Looking across the table at Edna, she said, "Ready to go?"

They settled their bill with the waiter and rose to confront the task ahead.

Chapter Eight

Twenty minutes later, as she and Peg approached Cherisse's room at the nursing home in West Warwick, Edna gently laid her hand on her friend's arm. "Shall I wait for you in the sitting room?"

The look Peg returned was one of near panic. "No. I need you with me, Ed. I'm not sure I can face her alone. You don't have to say anything, but I'll feel much braver if you're there." Taking hold of Edna's hand, she moved quietly, pulling Edna along behind her, and slowly peered around the half-opened door.

"May I help you?" A soft, melodious voice came from inside the room.

When Peg didn't move, Edna nudged her forward. If she were to join them and not wait in the lounge, she at least wanted to see those in the room and not simply the back of Peg's head.

The speaker was a woman Edna guessed to be about seventy and then adjusted the age by two years when she realized this must be Cherisse's daughter Renee. She was a slender woman with wispy, white hair cut boyishly short. Wearing a sea-green polo shirt and charcoal-gray woolen slacks, she looked prim seated in a chair by the bed. Edna watched Renee's expression turn from curiosity to puzzlement to slow recognition as her eyes moved from Peg's face to Edna's and quickly back to Peg. The book she'd been reading dropped to her lap.

A brief silence ensued during which Cherisse's daughter stared long and hard at Peg. Finally, she said, "You look like your mother." Only then did she shift her gaze to the woman on the bed. "Don't you think, so, Mama?"

Cherisse Froissard rested against a mound of pillows that seemed to be keeping her upright. Her skin had a grayish cast and her short, straight hair lay like a limp cap on her head, but her light blue eyes held an interest that belied the frailty of the body.

When Renee turned back to them, her eyes, a slightly darker shade than her mother's, were cool. "It's been a very long time, Peg. What brings you here?"

"I …" Peg started to speak, then faltered until Edna gently poked her in the back. "I came to visit Cherisse."

"Why? And who have you brought with you?" Renee nodded toward Edna as she frowned at Peg. Her voice hadn't risen, but it did hold a hint of animosity.

"Renee." The woman on the bed reached a shaky hand toward her daughter, her tone weak but admonishing. Her other hand lifted from the coverlet to beckon Peg. "Come closer, dear, so I can see you better. These old eyes aren't so good anymore."

The room was overly warm and small, filled by the single hospital bed, a narrow bedside table and two chairs. The unoccupied chair stood beside a long, narrow window that looked out onto a small patch of grass and beyond to another wing of the facility. On the side of the room opposite the window were two doors. One concealed a bathroom and the other a closet, Edna guessed.

Peg took the few steps to reach Cherisse's side and stood across the bed from Renee who continued to frown, but more in question than hostility now, it seemed to Edna. In contrast, Cherisse's smile was open and friendly.

"You *do* look like your mother, Peggy dear. She was very pretty, you know."

Peg didn't reply, but took the old woman's hand and held it between her own. Edna couldn't tell if Peg didn't know what to say or if she didn't trust herself to speak at the moment. Edna guessed it was the latter.

Silence filled the room until she wanted to say something if only to cut through what was growing to be an awkward embarrassment. Before she could think of what to say, however, Cherisse spoke, repeating her daughter's earlier words.

"It *has* been a long time. What brings you here today? Has Virginia told you I am dying?"

"Oh, no." Peg sounded shocked. "She hasn't said anything of the sort."

"What then? Why should you suddenly show up at my mother's bedside?" The questions burst from Renee harsh and loud. Glancing at her mother as if in apology, Renee softened her next words. "Mama isn't strong and tires easily. Please say whatever it is you came to say and then leave us."

"Renee," Cherisse rolled her head on the

pillow to scowl at her daughter in silent rebuke. Only a few heartbeats passed before her face brightened and she smiled. "My daughter means well. Takes care of me, but worries too much." She reached out to Renee and, as she did so, her eyes went to a small vase of yellow daffodils on the bedside table. "She grows such beautiful flowers. She brought these to me this morning." Cherisse swiveled her head on the pillow to look back at Peg. "Now, dear, tell us what has brought you here today."

"Actually, I came to show you something." Peg pulled the small box from her handbag, adding as she did so, "And I came to apologize."

"Apologize?" Cherisse's face showed surprise.

Renee glowered.

Edna watched as Peg set the small box on the bed near the withered hand she had released seconds before. Slowly, almost reluctantly, she removed the lid and took out the wad of tissue. She looked at neither of the Froissard women as she began to open the filmy white paper in the palm of her hand. All eyes were on the object, so only Edna realized another person had entered the room when he moved quietly to stand next to her.

"What's going on?" A deep, male voice cut into the silence of the room, making them all jump. "Having a party?" He looked around the room with an amused expression, waiting for someone to answer.

Edna saw Renee tilt her head in Peg's direction and guessed the stranger's identity before Cherisse's daughter confirmed it. "As you can see, Guy, Mama's got a visitor."

The tall, good-looking man with wavy gray hair was Cherisse's son. Guy slid his eyes to Edna. She guessed him to be about six feet tall, slender like his sister, with a thick moustache on his upper lip that was more pepper than salt. His eyes were a shade of blue nearly identical to his sister's, except his had a touch of humor that hers did not. Edna had the immediate impression that he considered himself quite the dandy. *With good reason*, she thought. His open-neck, pearl-gray silk shirt and black slacks were as neat and trim as the rest of his appearance.

She smiled faintly, nodded briefly and stared back until Guy finally shifted his eyes to Peg. It took him a few seconds longer than his sister to recognize his former childhood playmate. "Peggy?" His tone was a question, wonder and doubt in his voice. "Peggy Graystocking?" He shook his head in disbelief. "You look like Isabelle. What are you doing here?" The anger that had colored his sister's questions and comments wasn't apparent in his tone.

"Hello, Guy," Peg said quietly, staring steadily back at him.

"Sit down, please, Guy. She came to show me something." Cherisse's smile held a touch of annoyance at his interruption before she looked back anxiously at Peg's hands.

Instead of sitting, Guy moved to stand in front of the window. From behind his sister, he studied Peg curiously. Brother and sister looked very alike except where Renee appeared skeptical, Guy's expression held curiosity.

Peg looked down at her open palm, at the object resting in the paper. Edna noticed her take a deep breath before lifting the brooch by its backing and holding it out for Cherisse to see.

The old woman said nothing at first. She simply stared at the object in Peg's hand while the tiny clock on her bedside table ticked away the seconds. Then, what little color she had drained from her face, and Cherisse's eyes seem to roll back in her head as she fainted.

No more than two seconds elapsed before the room erupted into chaos. Renee stood abruptly, her book falling to the floor with a loud slap. She bent over her mother at the same time as she reached for the cord to summon a nurse. Guy hurried around to the other side of the bed, pushing Peg aside to bend over his mother and take her hand. There was no sign of humor in his eyes when he turned to glare at Peg.

"What have you done? What is that?" His gaze dropped to the pin she still held between thumb and finger.

Seeing her friend frozen in shock and horror, Edna walked quietly to Peg's side and took hold of her arm. "We should go," she whispered.

Peg grabbed the box and the tissue paper from the bed and jammed them into her purse. "I'm sorry. I'm so sorry," she said, staring at Cherisse's still form. "I had no idea ... I thought she'd be relieved."

"Get out," Renee hissed with suppressed

fury.

"You'd better go," Guy said, more kindly but just as firm.

At that moment, a middle-aged woman in a pink, button-down blouse and white slacks hurried into the room and inserted herself between Renee and the bed. "What's the trouble?" She spoke across Cherisse to Guy.

Wanting to get her out of the room, Edna tugged on Peg's wrist, noticing as she did so that Peg's hand was balled into a tight fist. She pulled Peg toward the door and out into the corridor. The walk to the parking lot seemed endless. In the car, fastening seatbelts, she thought to ask, "Do you have the brooch?"

Raising her fist, Peg slowly opened her fingers. She had been clutching the jewel so fiercely that the pin had jabbed into her palm and drawn blood.

"Oh, Ed. What have I done?" The question was filled with sorrow and humiliation.

Edna knew Peg wasn't talking about the bloody wound. She also knew that nothing she could say would help right then. Gently, she patted Peg's forearm, started the car and drove wordlessly back to Peg's house, feeling her friend's anguish as Peg silently stared out the side window.

When they reached the Graystocking mansion, Edna wasn't going to leave Peg to dwell on the events of the afternoon. Parking the car, she escorted her friend into the house and through to the kitchen, where they found Virginia sitting at the table, staring out at the back yard. She held a red rosary in her hands that she dropped hastily into her apron pocket when Edna and Peg walked into the room. "Are you alright, Mrs. Bishop," she asked, getting to her feet and eyeing Peg with concern.

"Would you get some antiseptic and bandages," Edna asked once they had explained how Peg had punctured her hand. Nothing was said about the visit to Cherisse.

Virginia had finished dressing Peg's wound and was gathering up bottles and bandages when Stephen strode into the room, speaking as he entered. "I won't be here for dinner tonight, Virginia. I'm ..." He stopped talking when he saw the group huddled around the table. "I didn't know you were home, Margaret. Hello, Edna." Coming closer to his wife, he saw the bandage and asked what she'd done.

"It's nothing," she replied. She'd left the brooch on the table so they could clean it with alcohol once they'd bandaged her hand.

As Stephen reached for the pin, Peg covered it with her undamaged hand and, without looking at him, said, "No, Stephen. I'm keeping this for now."

He glared at her for several seconds before turning to Virginia. "As I was saying, I won't be home for dinner." With that, he spun on his heel and left the way he'd come.

"I'd better be getting home." Edna was the first to speak and break the uneasy silence that had settled into the room. "First, though, I'd like to talk to your gardener, see if he has any questions about the plans we drew up for planting the herbs." Glancing at the wall clock, she noticed it was after five. "Will he still be working?"

Peg replied half-heartedly, "He was off today. He'll be back tomorrow. I'm sure he's following our blueprint."

"Just the same, Peg, if you don't mind, I'd like to talk to him sometime." Edna didn't want to voice her true reason in front of Virginia, that she wanted to question Goran to find out how much he actually knew about gardening.

Peg smiled weakly. "Will you ever forgive him for mistaking lemon balm for mint?"

"Well, for heaven's sake, everyone knows all you have to do is crush a leaf between your thumb and forefinger to smell the difference."

"Of *course* everyone knows that," The amusement in Peg's eyes looked genuine for the first time since they had entered the nursing home. "Well, if you don't mind the drive, come by and check on Goran whenever you'd like. He should be working the next two days."

Edna drove home with a myriad of images whirling around in her head. Cherisse's ghostly pallor, Renee's and Guy's fury, Peg's humiliation and Stephen's anger. As she reached South County and neared her own home, her thoughts turned to the conversation she'd had with Charlie that morning. On impulse, she turned up onto her neighbor's driveway. If Jaycee answered the door, Edna would invite her over for a glass of wine.

Chapter Nine

In fact, Jaycee was home but hesitated over Edna's invitation, at first. Thinking it was a natural shyness on the young woman's part, Edna said she would welcome the company since her husband was out of town and her daughter had returned to her condo in Boston. Odd, Edna thought, that Jaycee should seem relieved at the news. She accepted with pleasure and agreed to come over in a half hour, giving Edna time to prepare appetizers and open the wine.

After feeding Benjamin and letting him outside, Edna rummaged in the refrigerator for sour cream and cream cheese. She mixed equal parts of each before stirring in freshly chopped dill, chives and basil. Transferring the spread to a small Wedgewood bowl which she placed on a matching plate, she surrounded the dip with two varieties of homemade crackers and some celery sticks. She carried the food into the living room and set it on the coffee table along with cocktail napkins and was returning to the kitchen to fetch wine glasses when the doorbell rang. Her young neighbor was prompt.

Once they were settled on the gold brocade sofa, she attempted to put her guest at ease. "Jaycee's a pretty name. One I haven't heard before."

"Thank you. It's really sort of shorthand for my initials."

"Oh?" Displaying only polite curiosity, Edna was nonetheless pleased that one of her hunches had been correct. She tucked it to the back of her mind to let Charlie know.

"Yes. You see, I was named for my two grandmothers, Joanna and Charlotte. My parents didn't want to favor one grandmother over the other, so they called me by both names. When I started school, 'Joanna Charlotte' was too much of a mouthful, so the kids shortened it to my initials and it became a nickname, JAYcee."

Joanna, Edna thought. *I'm certain that was the name of the home buyer Charlie mentioned this morning. So the grandmother purchased the house.* Another bit of news to be tucked away for Charlie.

As Edna chatted with Jaycee, she found the young woman to be poised and intelligent but guarded. If her guest had any idea she was being pumped for information, Edna was certain she would lose the young woman's trust, so she tried to make her questions sound innocent.

"I detect a slight accent. Are you from the Midwest?"

"I have spent time there," Jaycee replied noncommittally. "What gives me away?"

"More of a guess on my part than anything. My sister lives in Chicago. Some of your speech reminds me of listening to her friends." Edna grinned mischievously as she admitted, "Besides, I recognized the area code on the envelope you dropped off last night."

Jaycee spread a cracker with the herb

mixture and took a thoughtful bite. Chewing, swallowing and taking a sip of wine before she spoke, she eventually shook her head. "Actually, I moved here from Florida. The phone number belongs to an old friend." She didn't look at Edna, but examined the plate of food instead, before selecting a celery stick. Her hesitation gave Edna the feeling that Jaycee thought she was revealing too much of herself. Still, Edna pushed to know more.

"Did you grow up in Florida?"

Jaycee merely nodded in reply. When she finally glanced over at Edna, a curious look narrowed her eyes, as if she were trying to decide something.

Edna was beginning to feel awkward at the young woman's reticence, but went on cheerfully with her chatter and her probing. After all, her questions were no more than anyone would ask when getting to know someone, she thought.

"Folks usually move to Florida from New England, not the other way around. What brought you to Rhode Island?"

"My mother's family was from Westerly. Her parents--my grandparents," Jaycee added unnecessarily, "moved to Florida when my grandfather retired. Gran's a widow. I stay with her sometimes." She sat back against the corner of the sofa. Holding her wine glass in two hands, she looked around the room. "Your home is very comfortable. I like antiques. Gran's house is filled with heirlooms, too."

Edna recognized the obvious change of

subject, but decided not to give up just yet. She was trying to figure out how to ask what Jaycee did for a living when her guest leaned forward and twirled a celery stick in the herb spread before taking a bite. "Hmmm. This is good. Did you make it?"

She definitely wants to get out of the limelight, Edna thought. "Yes," she said, "it's become a new interest of mine, experimenting with various herbs from my garden."

"Yum. I should pick your brain. I'm working on an idea for a cookbook."

"Really? What sort of cookbook?"

Jaycee's eyes sparkled and her face brightened with enthusiasm. "I want to put together authentic New England recipes and illustrate them with photographs of historic and scenic places along the coast. You know, sort of a gourmet travel guide. That's why I moved here, to work."

"What an interesting concept. Have you collected many recipes?"

"You bet. That's what gave me the idea. I have Gran's file box. It's crammed full of cards and scraps of paper, hers plus many from friends and relatives. She's also given me a few of her old cookbooks and those have notes all along the margins. Kind of fun to read, you know?"

Edna nodded and reached to spread a cracker for herself. Still determined to find out more information for Charlie, she said, "Your 'Gran' must be your mother's mother. From Westerly, did you say?"

"That's right."

"Does your father's family also come from this area?"

Before Jaycee could answer, the doorbell rang, causing her to jump and slop wine onto her navy slacks. She quickly grabbed a napkin from the coffee table to soak up the spill, but not before Edna saw worry in the young woman's eyes.

Hurriedly, she tried to reassure her guest. "I'm not expecting anyone. It's probably kids out selling something to earn money for school. I'll see who it is and be right back."

But when she opened the door, it wasn't local school children who'd come calling. Mary stood on the stoop, grinning down at her. Hank and Benjamin stood beside the tall redhead and stared up expectantly at Edna before the cat, followed closely by the dog, bounded past her and down the hall. Before Edna could utter a word, Mary, too, swept past her into the house. "Hi. Benjy came over to visit. Hank and I decided to walk him back home."

"Benjamin," Edna corrected automatically as she shut the door.

Undaunted, Mary went on, "Thought you could use some company since Al's out of town."

"Albert," Edna corrected, again automatically. One of these days, Mary might get the hint and use their full names. Knowing it would be difficult to send Mary home before she was ready to leave, Edna said dryly, "Won't you come in" and wondered if Jaycee would feel betrayed, since she had been assured they would be alone. *Oh well, nothing to be done but make introductions.*

As they approached the archway into the living room, Edna heard Jaycee talking to the animals. "What's your name, big fellow?" When she entered followed by Mary, Jaycee looked up with a laugh. She seemed not at all disturbed by having someone else join their little party. All the concern in her expression had evaporated. Hank sat at her knee, one paw on her thigh, and Benjamin stood on the sofa beside her.

"How adorable and friendly." She chuckled, patting the dog's head as she scooped the cat onto her lap.

Edna introduced the two neighbors, relieved that, for once, Mary looked fairly normal in white slacks and a lime-green jersey, one of her hospital volunteer costumes. Edna guessed Mary had not expected to meet Jaycee that evening, or she probably would have donned one of the Hawaiian-print caftans she wore for special occasions. As Edna's mind wandered through Mary's distinctive wardrobe, the red-head dropped into the mahogany arm chair at right angles to where Jaycee sat stroking Hank's back. "He's my buddy," Mary explained as Edna wheeled around to head toward the kitchen.

Carrying the wine bottle and a glass for Mary, Edna refilled Jaycee's glass and her own before reclaiming her place on the sofa. Her guests seemed to be having a pleasant time talking to and about the animals in the room. If Jaycee still had reservations about the person she'd described as "a little odd," she hid her feelings well.

Edna was beginning to fear she'd never get back to finding how Jaycee was connected to Chicago, when Mary piped up. "Where're you from?"

With a sigh, knowing she'd never control the conversation with Mary in the room, Edna sat back, sipped from her goblet and listened while Jaycee answered questions she'd already been asked. As Edna watched the other two, she realized how fortuitous Mary's arrival had been. With the animals and Mary vying for her attention, Jaycee finally seemed to relax.

While the women talked, Edna's thoughts were busy building on the seed of an idea Jaycee had planted in her head. As soon as she could politely interrupt, she explained to Mary, "Jaycee is compiling recipes and photographs for an illustrated New England cookbook."

Mary was an off-again, on-again cook who, when the urge took hold, threw together whatever ingredients grabbed her fancy. Oddly enough, her dishes were very tasty, in Edna's opinion. The two women had recently begun to compare notes and, once or twice, had even worked side-by-side. To date, these culinary events had taken place only in Mary's kitchen. Edna wasn't yet ready to share her space with someone who was apt to dirty every dish in the pantry and coat every working surface with bits of food.

She turned to Jaycee and nodded at the tray on the butler-style coffee table. "Mary made the crackers and cheese sticks you've been nibbling on this evening."

Jaycee's eyes widened as she turned to Mary who was looking as smug as the Cheshire Cat. "Did you really? These are delicious. Are they family recipes?" Her questions held obvious delight.

Blushing slightly at the praise, Mary said, "The basic recipes come from a little book called "Easy Homemade Crackers using Herbs" by Jim Long. Sometimes I try different herbs or a different flour, like rye instead of wheat."

"Wasn't it Mrs. Rabichek who got you interested in cooking with herbs?" Edna prompted, already knowing the answer.

"She gave me the idea," Mary admitted with a nod. Turning to Jaycee, she said, "I went online to look for herbs that Old Mrs. Rabichek didn't have in her garden, so I could get her something new. She was always looking for different stuff to try growing and experimenting with. I found the Long Creek Herb site and that's where I found this book on crackers. If you're looking for New England recipes, you gotta include crackers. They were invented in Newburyport, Massachusetts, you know, in the late seventeen hundreds. That's in Jim's book, too, a history of how crackers were discovered."

Edna thought she'd better cut in before Mary got too wound up and talked Jaycee's ear off. Distracting both guests by passing the hors d'oeurves plate, Edna spoke to Jaycee. "You said you have lots of recipes, but how about pictures?"

She wrinkled her nose and squinted in mock dismay. "That's the hard part. Since I've never lived here myself, I need to do some research. I bought a scooter so I could start roaming around and get a feel for the place. My other problem is that I don't take very good pictures." She now looked more self-conscious than dismayed. "I hope to find a good camera and practice. Hopefully, I'll come up with some useable photos."

Excitedly, Mary sat straighter in her chair and gaped at Edna. "You should introduce her to Starling."

Edna smiled, mentally thanking Mary for verbalizing the idea. "Just what I was thinking," she said.

Chapter Ten

Wondering how Albert was coping, Edna tried his cell number first thing the following morning. Her call went directly to voice mail.

"Drat," she muttered, looking at the receiver as if it were responsible for her husband turning off his phone or letting the battery run down. She was also concerned about Stan and wanted to know if he were any better and out of intensive care. She wondered if Bea had arrived and how she was handling her husband's sudden heart attack. Heaving a sigh of frustration, she left a brief message for Albert to call as soon as he got the chance.

She then phoned Charlie to report on the events and conversation of the previous evening. "At first, I thought Jaycee didn't like the idea of collaborating with a photographer, but that was probably my imagination. She might just be shy. Mary was the one who convinced her that Starling would be fun to work with."

Charlie was enthusiastic over the proposal. "You're great. That's exactly what I need, someone on the inside."

"You must do your part now," she reminded him. "I know my daughter well enough to assume she'll be glad to show Jaycee around and even help with the photography, but Starling's back in Boston because you said you'd be too busy to see her this week. Now you'll have to convince her to come back and stay for a while, if this plan is to work. I can't hang out with Jaycee. First of all, I'm too old, and secondly, I'm too busy."

"Leave it to me. I'll talk her around."

"How much will you confide in her?" Edna had to know what Charlie was going to tell Starling in order to keep her own story straight.

There was a pause on the line before he answered. "I don't think Starling is as good an actress ... "

Read "liar," thought Edna, appreciating Charlie's diplomacy.

" ... as you are. I'll say the case I'm on has turned out to be less complicated than we thought, and I have evenings free after all."

"She might not trust you after you stood her up the other night."

"Oh, I think I can persuade her."

From his tone, Edna could almost see his mischievous grin. She smiled herself as she replied, "I believe that's all I need to know for now. See you, Charlie." She heard his laugh as she hung up the phone.

She was still sitting at her desk, going over in her mind how she would introduce her daughter to Jaycee, when the phone rang. She saw from the caller id screen that it was Peg.

"Mornin'," Edna said with the broadest New England accent she could muster.

"Mornin'," came the equally heavy reply.

"What gets you out of bed so early on this

beautiful spring day?"

"Too much to do to laze around like the rich and pampered. Did I wake you?"

Edna couldn't help herself. She laughed. Peg had always been better at making Edna crack a smile than the other way round. Peg knew very well that Edna rose with the sun, if not before, while Peg was the night owl who, because she stayed up until one or two in the morning, generally slept in.

"Are you even out of bed yet," Edna asked with a glance at her watch. "It's barely eight o'clock."

"As a matter of fact, I've been up since seven this morning," Peg retorted with a touch of pride in her voice which immediately turned into little-girl excitement as she continued. "The Froissards are coming to lunch today. Oh, Ed, they've forgiven me, I'm sure of it. I feel as if a hundred-pound weight has been lifted from my shoulders."

"Whoa," Edna said, confused. "Back up. What's happened? They were practically spitting fire when we left Cherisse's room yesterday afternoon. I assume this news also means Cherisse has recovered and is feeling better?"

"Yes, she is. Virginia told me Cherisse is fine. Well," Peg hesitated, "as fine as she will ever be these days."

"Okay, Peg, start from the beginning." Edna sat back in her desk chair, figuring the call would be a long one.

"I know you said something about coming

to the house today to speak with Goran, so I thought I'd call and let you know that, according to Virginia, the Froissards want to see me. I've invited them to lunch. Do you mind interrogating Goran another time?" She paused briefly, then as if a new thought had occurred to her, said, "Or I could send him to you. Do you have something else I could tell him you're donating to the garden? I don't think I could tell him to drive down because you want to grill him, do you?"

"No. That probably wouldn't be wise," Edna replied wryly. She thought for a minute. "I could thin out my irises this morning. If I remember your designs, you could use some bulbs to plant along the fence on the south side of your yard."

"Perfect. I'll send him down this afternoon. Will that give you enough time?"

"I should be done by noon, so any time after that will be okay. Now, tell me about this lunch you're having with the Froissards. How did this come about?"

"After you left yesterday, I had a long talk with Virginia. I told her about showing Cherisse the brooch and how she'd fainted and how upset Guy and Renee had become. Well, you know Virginia. She took off and went to see for herself just how bad Cherisse was."

Edna heard relief calming Peg's voice as she talked and thought how fortunate it was that Virginia had not only stayed in touch with the Froissards, but was friendly enough with them to intercede on Peg's behalf. Her thoughts drifted back to what Peg was saying.

"... Cherisse had recovered and seemed no worse for what must have been a shock. Virginia must have scolded Renee and Guy. Said it was about time we buried the hatchet, since my parents were long gone and, after all, we once had been so close. She invited them to lunch, telling them it would be a good chance to talk things out."

"How do you feel? Are you nervous about seeing them alone? If you want me to lend you courage, I could still drive up with the excuse of talking with your gardener."

"Thanks, Ed. You are a brick, but I'm feeling better about visiting with them now that the worst seems to be over. They really were like an older brother and sister when I was growing up. Seeing them yesterday made me realize how much I have missed them. We've got a lot of catching up to do. I'm afraid we'd bore you to tears."

"Do you think they'll like Stephen?" Edna hoped her question sounded more diplomatic than she felt. "Would you be more comfortable meeting them in a neutral zone, like a restaurant?"

"Stephen probably won't even be home for lunch. Most days, he says he's too busy to stop for lunch. Besides, Virginia said Renee and Guy would like to see the place again. She told them about my plans to restore the gardens. I remember Renee loved working in the yard with my mother, so maybe she'll remember things that I've forgotten. I'll definitely show them my drawings."

Edna heard the happiness and relief in her friend's voice and was glad for Peg. "It sounds like you'll have a good visit. I'll want a full report," she said, only half teasing.

"You got it. Thanks for understanding, Ed. I'll talk to you soon." With that, Peg hung up, leaving Edna to hope the day would be as pleasant as Peg was expecting. Remembering the looks on the faces of both brother and sister, Edna wasn't encouraged. Hanging up her own phone, she shook her head, shrugged and rose to fetch her gardening tools.

An hour later, she, with Benjamin's assistance, was digging up iris bulbs in the middle of the circle inside the broken-shell driveway when Starling drove up in her eight-year-old, white Celica. Living in Boston, she knew better than to drive a new, an expensive or a coveted-model car. Chances were better than average in the city that a vehicle would suffer damage or be stolen or both. On the bright side, Bean Town was so compact that most people, Starling included, got around by a combination of foot power and public transportation.

"Back so soon?" Sitting back on her heels, Edna greeted her daughter with an innocent smile and a wave.

"Gary kicked me out." Referring to her business partner in the photography studio, Starling leaned out the car's window, her lower lip protruding in a mock pout. "He said I'm being totally useless, and he's tired of listening to me complain about my boyfriend."

"Is that what you've been doing?" Edna held onto her broad-brimmed straw hat with a gloved hand as she looked up at her daughter.

"I guess so. Anyway, I decided to return to
my original plan of spending a few days here. I
want to build up my photo inventory of places
around the Rhode Island shores. And guess what?"
Her face lit up while she continued chattering, not
waiting for Edna to respond. "Just as I was leaving
my condo, Charlie called to tell me he's not that
busy after all."

"That *is* good news, dear. Park your car
and come help me up, will you?" After sitting on
the ground for longer than she'd intended, Edna
felt her legs beginning to cramp.

When Starling was out of the car and Edna
was on her feet, she said, "Come with me. I want
you to meet our new neighbor. Her name is Jaycee
Watkins."

As they walked across the street and up the
slope to the front porch, Edna explained further.
"If you're going to be home for a few days *and*
out taking pictures, I think you can help Jaycee
with a special project she's doing--when you're
not with Charlie, of course. You and she are about
the same age, and I think you'll enjoy each other's
company."

"Oh?" Starling's curiosity was up, but not
without a hint of hesitancy and some humor.
"What are you getting me into now, Mom?"

Briefly and with growing enthusiasm over
the idea of the two young women collaborating,
Edna told Starling about Jaycee and her idea for
an illustrated cookbook. As they reached the porch
and she knocked on the door, Edna ended by

saying, "I thought you could start by taking her over to Carpenter's Mill in Perryville. She mentioned her grandmother's johnnycake recipe last night, so I thought, since it isn't far from here, she might like to see where the authentic Rhode Island flint corn meal comes from."

At Edna's knock, Jaycee opened the door almost immediately. She must have seen them crossing the narrow, country lane.

"This is my daughter, Starling, the photographer *extraordinaire* we told you about last night. My youngest and only unmarried child," Edna added.

"Don't mind my mother," Starling said, extending her hand. "She's still living in the dark ages where all women should be married and raising babies."

Taking Starling's hand, Jaycee said, "Gran feels the same way. I know the cross you bear."

The two laughed and Edna smiled, not at all bothered by her daughter's comeback and pleased that the young women seemed to like each other immediately. She wasn't easy about spying on Jaycee, but if the two hit it off, Starling would have someone nearby to pal around with when her latest love interest had to work. Since she'd begun to date a local police officer, Starling visited more often than she had since moving to Boston fifteen years ago, but it still wasn't often enough to suit either Edna or Albert. If Starling and Jaycee became friends and they learned more about each other in the process, it really wouldn't be like spying. Would it?

"Isn't that right, Mom?"

Edna was startled from her guilty thoughts by Starling's question. "I'm sorry, dear. What did you say?"

"I was telling Jaycee about your idea to go over to Perryville this afternoon." Starling frowned as if wondering where her mother's mind had strayed. "I said Carpenter's has been a working mill since the early seventeen hundreds."

"Yes, that's right. It's also the only water powered mill currently operating in Rhode Island."

"That sounds like the perfect place to begin collecting pictures and learning some history of the area. It's so nice of you to invite me." Jaycee's brown eyes shone with eagerness.

"My pleasure. I've come down from Boston to do some shooting anyway, so it'll be fun to have company."

After Starling and Jaycee agreed on a time to meet, the two Davies women headed back to the house. Once they were out of earshot, Starling said, "Didn't you say her name was Jaycee Watkins?"

"That's right," Edna smiled. "Why?"

"Oh, nothing. It's just that she looks familiar, but I don't recognize the name."

"I don't know how you could have met if she's just moved here from Florida. She probably reminds you of someone else you know." Edna dismissed the idea and said, "Why don't you take your suitcase upstairs and unpack. I have a call I need to make and then you can help me decide what to have for lunch."

As soon as Starling disappeared up the stairs with her suitcase and camera equipment, Edna ducked into the small office, shut the door quietly and punched in Charlie's cell phone number.

"I think our plan is going to work," she said in a near whisper. "The two hit it off and are spending the afternoon at Carpenter's Mill."

"That's good." Charlie sounded pleased and added before he hung up, "I'm taking Starling to dinner tonight. I'll look forward to hearing all about her new friend."

When Edna opened the office door, she was startled to see Starling standing on the other side. "You're being awfully secretive. What's going on? Is there something you're not telling me?"

Edna could feel guilt heat her cheeks, but said as innocently as she could manage, "I don't know what you mean?"

Starling put an arm through Edna's as they turned toward the front door. "Just that I've rarely known you to close the door to your office. Makes me wonder if you've got a secret pal."

Edna said in a conspiratorial whisper, "Don't tell your father."

Laughing--one with relief and the other over what she took as a joke--they walked out into the mid-morning sunshine to where Edna had left her gardening gloves. As she picked them up and put them on, another idea occurred to her. "Why don't you go ask Jaycee to join us for lunch? Tell her we're having my mother's fish chowder with corn bread. I'll even donate the recipe, if she will give Mother credit in her book."

"Yum. I love Gramma's chowda," Starling said with the typical New England pronunciation. She set off on her errand while Edna resumed thinning out the iris bed. With everything else going on, she had completely forgotten Goran Pittlani would also be arriving that afternoon.

Chapter Eleven

Edna was finishing her morning's chore, having filled a large paper grocery bag with iris bulbs, when Hank came bounding up, wagging his tail and panting as if he'd been running hard. As usual, Mary wasn't far behind. Starling, who had returned with Jaycee's enthusiastic acceptance of the invitation to lunch, was sitting on Edna's low garden stool, watching her mother work.

"Hi. Whatcha doin'?" Mary's typical greeting to Edna was followed by "Hi, Starling."

"Hi, Mary."

Edna mentally calculated that she'd have enough chowder to feed everyone if she took two containers out of the freezer. She knew by now that it would be easier to invite Mary to stay for lunch than to get her to go home, and then realized it would be wise to include her, making lunch a cozy, female foursome. The curious redhead would be less dangerous if she weren't left to use her imagination when telling other townsfolk about the new arrival to their community. Edna thought with both fondness and amusement how important it was to Mary for her to know the latest news.

"Have you seen a little black cat around?" As she spoke, Mary scanned the yard, obviously on the lookout for the feline.

"No," Edna said, unable to keep from glancing around herself. "Why? Is it yours?"

Mary's parents had never allowed her to have a pet, complaining she'd lose interest and they'd be left to care for the dog or cat or fish or whatever other oddity Mary would bring home. Now, in her mid fifties, after adopting Hank from his deceased owner's family, Mary had become so enamored of dogs and cats that she was visiting as many local animal rescue groups as she could find.

"Not mine. I've seen it a couple of times in the past week. She looks like she's only half-grown. Course, I'm not sure it's a 'she.' I think someone dropped it off at the side of the road to let it either fend for itself or get run over." She made a face to show how disgusted she was over such behavior. "I've been putting food out on the back porch for her for the last couple of days. It's always gone the next morning, so I think she's beginning to hang around and trust me."

"How do you know something else isn't eating the food," Starling asked, "like a raccoon or a fox or something?"

"I don't. But the kitten is still around. Saw her from my window this morning. She ran this way and disappeared behind your side of the stone wall."

"We'll keep an eye out for her," Edna promised. "Maybe Benjamin will make friends with her."

"That'd be nice," Mary's face brightened with the prospect before she frowned with curiosity at the bag Edna had just handed to Starling. "Whatcha goin' to do with all the bulbs?"

"They're for a friend." The question brought Goran to Edna's mind, and she wondered with a sinking feeling if he would show up while they were having lunch. She'd told Peg that he could come by after noon, but they hadn't agreed on a definite time. She wouldn't be able to question him thoroughly with others around. Mentally, she shrugged, deciding she couldn't worry about it.

In the kitchen, she heated the fish chowder, adding milk during the last few minutes. Starling mixed up yellow meal and baked cornbread in her great grandmother's cast iron pan with cups shaped like tiny corn cobs. Edna briefly thought of making bread pudding, another old New England recipe, but decided it would be too heavy a dessert and ended up washing a bunch of seedless grapes to serve with homemade sugar cookies.

After Jaycee arrived and the women were seated around the kitchen table, talk revolved around recipes and ideas for the illustrated cookbook.

"What about a cranberry bog," Jaycee asked. "A picture of cranberries would be a 'must' for this sort of book, wouldn't it?"

"Definitely," Starling said, buttering a piece of corn bread, "but that'd be better done in the fall. Foliage in the swamps and bogs are the first to change color. I have some shots back at the studio you can look at sometime."

"If you're travelin' up the coast," Mary said after swallowing a spoonful of chowder, "you should go to Deer Isle, Maine. It's a bit far north, but if you're including a finnan haddie recipe, you should see the smoker Stonington Seafood has for the haddock. It's a kiln the company shipped from Scotland a few years ago, and they say it's an exact replica of the first mechanized kiln."

"Oh, right," Starling agreed. "I've heard about that. It's called a Torry kiln. The original was built in Aberdeen, Scotland, in the late nineteen thirties."

Putting down her soup spoon and joining the conversation, Edna said, "That wouldn't be far from Bar Harbor. I think that whole area of Maine around Acadia National Park would be fun for Jaycee to see, if she's never been before." She turned to Jaycee. "Acadia was the first national park to be created east of the Mississippi."

"I'm going to have to start a list," Jaycee said with a laugh. "It's beginning to sound like I might be biting off more than I can chew, if you'll pardon the pun." She grinned widely at the others' groans and ducked when Mary threw a wadded-up paper napkin at her from across the table.

Chatter stopped for a few minutes while the only sounds were those of spoons clicking against bowls and knives clacking onto plates as the women ate. Finishing her chowder first, Starling resumed the conversation. "You could compile a good-sized cookbook for the Boston area alone," she said, settling back in her chair with a sigh. "That was delicious, Mom. Thanks for lunch."

Smiling and bowing her head slightly to acknowledge the compliment, Edna stood to clear away soup bowls and bread plates and replace them with dessert dishes. She set a bowl of grapes and a plate of cookies on the table before resuming her seat and turning to Jaycee. "Listening to all these suggestions, I think it might be a good idea for you to sit down with your recipes and a map and plot your course." Glancing at her daughter, she added, "Starling has been all over New England with her camera, so she should be able to help."

"Sure," agreed Starling. "I'll be glad to. Good idea to break up the writing and cooking with field trips, beginning this afternoon with Carpenter's Mill. Ready, Jaycee?" The two younger women rose and, chattering away, departed through the mudroom.

Intent on finding the little stray kitten, Mary and Hank left soon after, and Edna spent the rest of the afternoon puttering in the yard, weeding and loosening soil in the gardens with a hand rake. The afternoon sped by, and she was dusting off a few decorator pots, arranging them around the patio, when she heard the sputtering of a small engine coming from the front of the house. Curious as to what was making the noise, she hurried along the brick path to the driveway.

"Hello," called Jaycee as she put her foot down on the broken shells to balance the scooter.

"Well, hello," Edna greeted. She walked around examining the little red machine. "What a pretty bike." Then, frowning and looking toward the road, she said. "Is Starling with you?"

"Nah. She's gone to meet Charlie. She

dropped me off at home and was going to swing by here, but I told her I had some shopping to do and would come over and let you know. She seemed anxious to get going before Charlie changed his mind." Jaycee laughed. "I guess he must have to cancel their dates pretty often."

Edna chuckled in agreement. "If her luck holds, she won't be home for dinner tonight."

"I hope you're right. She seems to like him a lot." Changing the subject, Jaycee said, "I'm on my way to the grocery store. Is there anything I can pick up for you?"

"It's nice of you to ask. Come inside for a minute while I check my list. If you have time, I'll make some tea and you can tell me what you thought of the mill."

"Oh, wow," Jaycee exclaimed as she lowered the kickstand on her scooter, dismounted and took off her bicycle-style helmet. "That is such an interesting place. A picture of the grist mill will be great for my book. Thanks. I'm so glad you thought of it."

Edna was about to ask if Starling took her to any other sites or beaches along the coast when another two-wheeled vehicle turned in from the road. This one's engine, however, was loud enough to drown out all other sounds as it rounded the circular drive and pulled up next to them. The two women stood and stared as the black-leather clad man dismounted and removed his Darth Vader headgear. Goran Pittlani balanced the helmet on the seat of his motorcycle before coming forward.

"Hi." Ignoring Edna for the moment, he stared beyond her with frank admiration at Jaycee. "Goran Pittlani," he said with a courtly bow in her direction. Staring at her, he frowned slightly. "Have we met before?"

Jaycee shook her head. The smile on her lips left her eyes, but her tone was pleasant enough when she replied. "I'm sure we haven't. I'm Jaycee Watkins. Nice to meet you."

"Goran gardens for a friend of mine," Edna said, making further introductions. "Jaycee is a new neighbor." She turned to study Goran's vehicle. "I don't understand why you don't use a pickup instead of this thing." His mode of transportation only added to her doubts that he was any sort of gardener.

When he laughed, his dark eyes twinkled and vertical ridges deepened on either side of his mouth. "I do okay with my bike. When I need something bigger, I rent it." He turned back to Jaycee, motioning to her scooter with a nod of his head. "What's it going to be when it grows up?"

Despite her concerns about the gardener, Edna couldn't help chuckling as Jaycee retorted with a hint of playful annoyance, "Hey, my little Jenny suits me just fine."

"Jenny?" Goran's expression held both curiosity and amusement.

"Yes, 'Jenny.' You know, as in donkey. She's hard working and dependable." Jaycee's mouth clamped shut as if she'd said all she was going to on the subject.

"Donkey. Right," was Goran's reply.

Edna thought it was time to interrupt their banter, entertaining as it was. She was also eager to question Goran. "I was about to make tea. Would you like to join us?"

"My pleasure." His look in Jaycee's direction gave emphasis to his words.

Edna invited them to sit at the kitchen table while she put on the kettle and arranged a plate of blueberry muffins and sugar cookies, leftovers from breakfast and lunch. As she moved between table and counter, she listened to Goran ask some of the same questions Jaycee had been answering the evening before, so she listened with only half an ear until Jaycee turned interrogator.

"Are you from around here," she asked him as Edna brought a tray to the table.

"Here, let me help you." Goran half rose and held out his hands.

"I've got 'em." Edna had the feeling his action was more to avoid answering than to be polite, so she repeated the question as she took her seat. "I was wondering the same thing, Goran. I haven't detected an obvious accent."

"I'm from lots of places. We traveled all over when I was growing up," was all he offered as he accepted a cup of tea.

"Was your father in the military," Jaycee asked, choosing a muffin from the plate in the middle of the table.

"Army." Goran's offhand reply was followed immediately by a smile as he finally raised his eyes from the sweets to meet Edna's gaze. "I haven't had homemade blueberry muffins in years. These look fresh, but this isn't blueberry season, is it?"

"July, usually," Edna agreed, mentally ticking off another black mark against this man who was posing as a gardener, but had to ask about growing seasons. She decided to ask the question foremost on her mind. "Have you been a gardener long?"

"Not really. Actually, I consider myself more of a general laborer, at this point. I'm learning, trying to work my way up to professional status." His boyish smile charmed her, and the frankness of his answer surprised her.

"What does that mean, exactly?" Jaycee frowned, joining in the conversation.

As soon as she'd spoken, Goran bit into his muffin and took a minute to chew, swallow and take a sip of tea before speaking. "I dig and plow and plant things where I'm told," he said to Jaycee with his disarming grin. "Not much expertise in it, but I don't mind. I get plenty of fresh air and exercise."

The little tea party passed in the same manner for another half hour. Once her guests had gone, Jaycee to buy groceries and Goran to return to Providence with the iris bulbs, Edna sighed, realizing she'd learned nothing of significance about either one. Disappointed, she wanted desperately to talk to Charlie to find out if he had any news, but she knew Starling would never forgive her if she interrupted what little time her daughter had with her policeman.

To relieve her frustration and satisfy the

need to speak with someone, Edna tried Albert's cell phone again. As before, she was connected immediately to voice mail. She left a brief message that she hoped sounded more upbeat than she was feeling and wondered if he were in consultation with Stan's doctors or if he'd simply forgotten to recharge his phone.

Moving to the living room, she switched on the television to watch the evening news, but the only tidbit that distracted her mind from her recent guests was the weather forecast, predicting a storm blowing in and bringing rain for the next day. *Good for the lawn and gardens*, she thought. Still restless, she decided to drive down to Matunuck Beach. A walk along the sandy shore would help tire her physically and maybe allow her to sleep. Otherwise, she knew she wouldn't relax until she'd had a chance to discuss with Charlie all the questions going around in her head, whether or not he had any answers.

She strolled along the beach for an hour and, when she finally did go to bed and was able to fall asleep, it was only to be awakened by the ringing phone. Struggling up from a sound sleep, she squinted at her bedside clock. "'ello," she slurred, wondering who in the world would be calling at 1:16.

So panicky was the voice on the other end of the line that she almost didn't recognize it as belonging to Peg.

"Ed, something terrible has happened. Virginia's dead."

Chapter Twelve

Edna was stunned, shaken fully awake in an instant. Holding the phone to her ear, she'd heard what Peg said, but couldn't quite believe it. She was speechless.

"Ed?" Peg's voice, still unnerved, rose to a near shrill. "Ed, are you there? Speak to me. Say something."

Finally, Edna said, "I'm here, Peg, but I don't know what to say. Try to calm down. Take a few deep breaths and tell me what happened. Can you do that?"

She listened to the faint sounds of Peg's breathing for nearly half a minute. When her friend spoke again, she still sounded anxious but more composed.

"After lunch with Renee and Guy this afternoon, Virginia said she wasn't feeling well and went upstairs to lie down. I told her to take an antacid and that I would clean up the kitchen. I didn't want her worrying about it. You know how she is."

Edna agreed as to how conscientious Virginia was, or had been. "Were Renee and Guy still with you?"

"Oh," Peg said, sounding as if she'd forgotten them and, after a slight pause as if to remember, said. "No. They left before Virginia said anything about feeling queasy. Stephen had gone back to work, too."

"Stephen? Was he at lunch with you?"

"Yes. He almost never comes home before six in the evening, but apparently he needed something from his desk here at the house. He was surprised to find I had guests. Of course I introduced him to the Froissards, and then there was all this explaining to do about how we grew up together. I hoped he'd remember it was their mother who had been accused of stealing the brooch we found the other day and not say anything embarrassing. He's been so obsessed about that pin, I was afraid he'd mention it." Her voice began to quiver with stress, so she stopped talking to take a deep breath before continuing. "I expected him to go back to work once he'd said hello. I still can't believe he decided to stay and eat with us. Thank goodness, Virginia always prepares more than enough food."

"If he came home at that hour, he probably would have expected to stay for lunch with you, wouldn't he?"

"Well, yes, I supposed he might have thought so, but I was certain he'd change his mind when he found I had company. He's never been comfortable with strangers."

Or with people he knows, Edna thought, remembering how withdrawn Stephen was whenever she and Albert spent time with the Bishops. At parties, he usually searched out a quiet corner. Around a dinner table, he concentrated on his food and made only the most cursory comments to anything his dinner partners said. As a result, the Bishops' friends who still invited them to parties learned to talk over and around him. "How did he behave with the Froissards?" Edna was very curious over Stephen's apparent behavioral about-face.

"Fortunately, he was attentive to everything that was said and even joined in the conversation occasionally. Can you believe it?"

Sensing her friend had calmed down enough to return to the main reason for her call, Edna refrained from commenting on Peg's rhetorical question and said hesitantly, "So, you and Virginia were alone when she went to her room to rest?"

"Alone in the house, yes. Goran was in the yard, of course. He'd come in earlier for his lunch, about an hour before he left to drive down to your place. Virginia ate in the dining room with us."

"But you say she's dead?" Edna's remark came out as a question. She was still having trouble believing she'd heard correctly. "What happened?"

"I don't know." Peg's voice began to rise with emotion again.

"Slow down," Edna warned. "Deep breaths, remember."

Obediently, Peg again took several seconds before resuming in a calmer, but still slightly quivering voice. "When she hadn't come downstairs by five thirty, I went up to check on her." she paused again to take several shaky breaths. "She looked awful and apparently had spent most of the afternoon in the bathroom. She complained of stomach cramps, so I got her another antacid. I made soup for dinner and brought her some on a tray. She said she still felt too nauseous to even look at it."

"Did you call a doctor?"

"She didn't want one. She said she was sure she'd be okay, just a bit of stomach flu, and not to bother." Peg began to sob. Through her tears, she said, "Oh, Ed, I shouldn't have listened to her. I should have called her doctor."

"Don't kick yourself, Peg," Edna said sternly. "You weren't to know."

Slowly, Peg's sniffles subsided. "I didn't check on her again until I went up to bed after the eleven o'clock news. That's when I found her." Peg wasn't crying, but it was a full minute before she managed to squeak out. "It was horrible."

Edna waited helplessly for a long minute. When Peg still hadn't said anything, Edna asked, "Where's Stephen? Isn't he with you?" She assumed Peg wouldn't be on the phone if her husband were with her and wondered why he wasn't holding her, trying to soothe away her grief.

"He's at the police station," came the tremulous reply.

Edna was confused. "The police station?"

"Yes. When I found her, I phoned nine-one-one. The police showed up a few minutes before the ambulance arrived. After the medical team confirmed Virginia was dead and took her away, the police said they needed a statement. Stephen volunteered to go down to the station to answer their questions. He didn't tell them that I was the one who found her. I stayed home to clean up her room. She had been horribly sick."

"Was Stephen with you when you found her?"

"No. He was downstairs in his office, working on some papers he needed for a meeting."

Edna was curious as to why Stephen would go to the police station, then realized he might have done so to get them out of the house, to give Peg some peace. *Maybe he has a heart after all*, she thought. Aloud, she said, "Would you like me to come stay with you?"

"That's kind of you, Ed, but Geoff is on his way over. I called him before I phoned you and he insisted on coming immediately. Fortunately, his room is always ready for guests or I'm afraid he'd be sleeping on the floor."

Speaking of her son's eminent visit seemed to have calmed Peg further. Enough so that Edna thought she could talk more about what had happened that evening. "I suppose it's too early to speculate what caused her death. Did they tell you when they'd expect to have the autopsy results?"

"They didn't say, but I heard one of the police officers mention food poisoning. That can't be, though." Peg took a deep, ragged breath before starting again, but seemed to be gaining control of herself. "The police asked what we had eaten and if we'd all had the same thing. I told them yes, as far as I know. Do you suppose they think I'm hiding something because neither Stephen nor I feel sick?" She stopped speaking, and Edna could hear her breathing deeply and slowly.

"The questions are simple routine, I'm certain," Edna said with conviction. She was wondering what else she could say to reassure her friend when Peg spoke up.

"Here's Geoff now. I must go. Thank you for being you, Ed, and for listening to me."

Before she hung up, Edna had time only to say, "Call me, if you need anything."

Just as she put the receiver back into the cradle of the bedside phone, a bolt of lightning lit the room like a giant flashbulb going off. The blinding light was followed in three heartbeats by a crack of thunder so loud, Edna jumped. She was throwing back the covers to get out of bed when she saw a small shadowy figure dart through the door and across the carpet to disappear beneath the bed. Benjamin slept in the mudroom off the kitchen and was not usually allowed upstairs, but she didn't say a word, knowing he'd feel comforted being near her while the storm raged outside.

She swung her feet off the bed and stood. Putting on her long velveteen robe, she cinched it around her waist as she walked to the window. The wind was pelting raindrops against the glass panes. As she watched from her second-floor window, another second-long flash of lightning illuminated the entire neighborhood. At that moment, she happened to be looking across at Jaycee's house. When she saw a dark figure standing in the center of the driveway, her hand flew to her mouth, stifling an involuntary scream. It looked like a man and it looked like he was walking toward the steps to the front porch.

Immediately, she thought of dialing 911. Then she wondered if she should call Charlie instead. What if it wasn't a man? What if it were Jaycee walking up to her house? No. Edna had seen the figure for a full second and, whoever it was, seemed larger than Jaycee. Considering for a moment, Edna thought of Mary. No, it hadn't been her either. The figure had looked to be broader than Mary. Perhaps as tall, since Mary was nearly six feet, but she was lanky, not broad and muscular. The person in the driveway had been a fairly large man.

These thoughts sped through Edna's mind as she remained staring out the window. Another flash of lightning, as bright and as long as the last, showed only an empty driveway. The figure had vanished.

Unsure what to do, Edna stood for another few minutes, watching as the lightning periodically spotlighted the neighborhood. Booming thunder that followed each pulsing glow of light did nothing to settle her nerves as she squinted through the rain-spattered window, trying to glimpse any movement outside the house across the street. Who would be walking around on a night like this? Should she call the police? Should she get Charlie out of bed for something that could turn out to be nothing at all? When eventually the lightning wasn't as bright and the accompanying thunder not as deafening, Edna gave up trying to see through the darkness. The storm was moving off and as the world outside quieted, so did her nerves.

Still, knowing she would be unable to sleep, she left her room and was heading for the stairs when the door to Starling's room opened and her daughter shuffled out in flannel pajamas and large, fluffy red slippers. With a wide yawn, she said, "Did the thunder wake you, too? What time is it, anyway?"

"Between half past one and two o'clock, I think. I'm going to make myself a cup of tea. Would you like some?" Edna thought briefly of telling Starling about the figure she'd seen, but decided not to frighten her. Besides, she wasn't even certain what exactly she'd seen or whom. She'd check on Jaycee at a more reasonable hour and make certain her neighbor was okay.

"Tea at this hour? No way," her daughter muttered, before turning around and stumbling back into her room. "G'night, Mom."

Smiling at the memory Starling had invoked of a sleepy-headed girl of six, Edna padded down the stairs and into the kitchen. Benjamin scooted past her and jumped onto the seat of a kitchen chair to settle down and watch as she filled the electric kettle with water and turned it on. Even with rain sheeting the windows, enough light shown from the street lamp to give adequate brightness to the room, so it wasn't until she'd started the kettle that she reached for the light switch and flicked it on. Almost immediately, she shut it off again. On the slim chance someone was wandering around in the downpour, she didn't want to be on display in a brightly lighted room.

While the water heated, Edna absently took a tea bag and put it into her favorite mug. In a few minutes, she added boiling water and stood at the kitchen sink, dunking the bag up and down while she gazed out the window at the dark, sodden night. Her mind was turning from an image of the figure in the driveway to one of Peg and Virginia. As her thoughts began to calm and settle on one mental picture, it was of Virginia in the Bishops' kitchen. Virginia preparing meals. Virginia sitting at the kitchen table. Virginia sipping a cup of tea. Virginia sliding red rosary beads through her fingers. Different times, different images, but all of the same stout woman in the Bishop's kitchen. What could have happened that she was now dead? She'd referred to a weak heart, but she'd certainly seemed healthy enough when Edna last saw her two days ago. Another picture flashed unbidden through Edna's head. Virginia slipping a sparkling brooch of red-white-and-blue gems into her apron pocket.

Images brought questions, both roiling in her head as Edna finished her tea and wandered back to bed. Tossing and turning, she dozed fitfully for the next few hours and was startled awake at 4:36 by the sound of tires crunching the broken shells on the driveway. Automobile noises were followed by a thwack against the front door. "Newspaper," she murmured into her pillow and relaxed. The wind had died down, and she listened to the gently falling rain for the next twenty minutes before finally deciding she wasn't going to get any more sleep, exhausted as she was.

Donning her robe, she plodded down the stairs and opened the front door. The newspaper was lying in a puddle and, although bagged, it was soaked through. When she picked it up, she noticed a square of paper lying on the stoop. Picking that up also, she realized it had been a hand-written note, until the water had made a mess of the ink.

She dumped the newspaper into the recycle bin, knowing it was too wet to bother reviving. Before tossing the note in with it, she looked more closely and decided to let it dry out. Laying it on the kitchen counter atop a piece of paper towel, she then started the coffee and took eggs and bacon out of the refrigerator. She'd let Starling get her own breakfast whenever she got up. Edna hadn't heard her come in the night before, so couldn't guess when her daughter would rise.

Awakened by Edna's early morning activities, Benjamin jumped off the chair where he'd spent the rest of the night. He took a long stretch with front paws extended and fanny in the air. He then walked to his water bowl and lapped while waiting for Edna to add a dry breakfast treat to his food dish.

Only when she'd finished feeding the cat and herself and rinsed the dishes did she examine the white square of paper with its abstraction of blue ink. The message seemed to begin with "Go..." The next letter looked like it could be either an "n" or an "r" but it was hard to decipher since the rest of the word had smeared. The middle part of the note was a blur of blue ink, looking more like finger painting than words. Only a bit of the last word and the letter "J" were visible at the bottom of the sheet. The last recognizable scribble was "...rry" and Edna guessed the "J" was the beginning of Jaycee's signature. She couldn't think of anyone else whose name began with J who would have left a note on the front door.

She wondered when and why Jaycee would have left the message, but decided to wait until a decent hour before walking across the street to ask the young woman herself. With her head filled with an image of a dark figure on the rain-slicked driveway, Edna thought she would also use the note as an opportunity to check on her neighbor's welfare and ask if she'd had a midnight visitor.

Chapter Thirteen

Edna was restless. She wanted to talk to Charlie and to Albert, and, most of all, to Peg, but it was too early to phone any of them. Ordinarily, she would have spent an hour or so reading the paper and doing the crossword puzzle, but that was out of the question this morning. Even if the paper weren't a soggy mess, she wouldn't have been able to concentrate. Too many thoughts were swirling in her head. She went back upstairs to shower and dress for the day, mentally reviewing what she could remember of the middle-of-the-night conversation she'd had with Peg. Edna found it nearly impossible to believe Virginia was dead.

By the time she returned downstairs, the wind had picked up again, whipping tree branches against each other as if in a frenzied fencing match. It would be a good day to stay home, but she was too restless to relax. She thought she might drive to Providence later to be with Peg, find out more about what had happened the afternoon before and maybe even have a chance to speak with Goran again. In the meantime, she paced around the house, watching the storm through the windows, first to the north, then to the west. She was in the kitchen, staring out the east-facing window above the sink when Starling came downstairs. She was dressed in fitted jeans and a yellow sweatshirt. Her auburn hair was pulled back into a pony tail. She looked as she had when she'd been about fifteen years old, but even that pleasant memory couldn't relieve Edna's anxieties.

"What's wrong, Mom? You're pacing around like a caged lion. I could hear you from my room."

"Sorry, dear. Did I wake you?" She was still distracted, unable to settle down mentally or physically. Uncertain over how to break the news of Virginia's death to her daughter, she thought briefly of delaying the task by asking Starling about her afternoon with Jaycee, but that topic didn't seem very important in light of everything else that was happening.

She was saved from having to make an immediate decision by a loud rapping at the back door. Mother and daughter looked at each other in alarm for a second before relaxing. "Mary," they agreed in unison. The synchronized response made them laugh, and Edna felt the tension in her neck and shoulders ease slightly.

"Let her in, would you, dear? I'll make coffee. I'm sure you and she could use a hearty breakfast, too."

Moments later, Hank followed Starling into the kitchen and Mary brought up the rear. As usual when the outside humidity was high, Mary's rust-red hair surrounded her head like a bushy lion's mane.

"Whatcha doin'?"

Edna started to smile at the familiar greeting, but stopped when she saw the forlorn look on Mary's face. Ordinarily, her neighbor would have been just the distraction the doctor would have ordered, but not this morning. "What's wrong," she asked. "What are you doing out and about in this weather?"

"Thought I'd look for the little black kitten. She might be scared or soaked or both after that storm last night. She didn't eat any of the food I put out for her last night."

"She probably found a place to keep dry and didn't want to leave it for food." Edna spoke with confidence, trying to be reassuring.

"Hope so." Head down, Mary moved to the table and rested her hands on the back of a chair.

"Come on, Mary, cheer up. The kitten will be fine. You'll see." Starling moved to give Mary a one-arm hug and pulled out the chair next to the one Mary was clutching. "I could use some coffee. How about you?"

Mary looked at her, returned the hug and nodded. Her expression began to brighten. "Sure. That'll be nice."

Learning that Mary hadn't had breakfast yet, Edna insisted that she and Starling sit, drink their coffee and keep out of her way while she set about frying bacon, scrambling eggs and toasting crumpets. More of the early morning's tension left her shoulders as she moved about the kitchen.

Hank flopped down on the floor near Mary's chair. Benjamin materialized to sniff the dog's wet, black coat, after which the ginger cat sneezed in disgust and leapt onto his favorite cushioned chair to nap. Head on his outstretched paws, Hank did nothing but follow Benjamin with his eyes before raising them in adoration to his mistress' face.

"What's the good word?" Mary said to Starling before taking a sip of coffee.

"Dunno. Something's going on with Mom this morning, but I haven't gotten it out of her yet."

Both stared expectantly at Edna as she brought their breakfasts to the table. After refilling coffee mugs, she sat across from them.

"Eat before it gets cold," she advised. "Then I'll fill you in." She suspected that neither of them would have much of an appetite once they heard what she had to report. Besides, she could use the time to organize her thoughts.

Eventually, unable to think of any gentle way to break the news of a death, she approached the topic head on. "Your Aunt Peg phoned in the middle of the night," she began when Starling and Mary had finished eating and were settled back in their chairs. "Peg has been my best friend since we met as freshmen in college," she explained to Mary in an aside. "She found her housekeeper dead yesterday evening." Edna waited a minute for the news to sink in before she went on. "They think it might be food poisoning, but Peg had some people in for lunch--a lunch Virginia prepared herself--and apparently nobody else has suffered ill effects. I don't have all the details, but I can't imagine how something like that could have happened, not in their home."

"I can't either." Starling sat forward. "Virginia kept one of the cleanest kitchens in the world. I always thought she was borderline manic about food preparation."

"You gonna investigate?" Mary looked curiously at Edna. "Like you did when Tom died," she added, reaching down to stroke Hank when he lifted his head at the mention of his former owner. Tom had been a friend of Mary's since her high school days. Less than a year before, he had been poisoned. Mary had adopted the black Labrador when Tom's daughter couldn't take him.

Edna shook her head in answer to Mary's question. "Nobody's saying she was deliberately poisoned. Even if she were, I'm sure the police wouldn't appreciate someone like me suggesting anything different--or butting into their business. Peg was upset last night, with good reason. I'll phone her later this morning to see how she's doing. She might be able to tell us a little more about what happened."

"Not to change the subject," Starling said, changing the subject. "But Mary just reminded me of something I've been meaning to ask you. Have you ever told Dad about your adventures, or should I call them *misadventures*?"

"No, and don't either of you ever breath a word to him," Edna said sternly. She felt her stomach go hollow at the thought of Albert learning that his wife had twice been drawn into solving a crime and, both times, had been threatened at gun point. There was no reason to alarm him after the fact. What was done couldn't be undone, and Edna had no intention of putting herself in that sort of danger again.

"Aren't you gonna help your friend?" Mary looked disappointed. Typical of the kind-hearted, well-meaning woman, she went on the alert whenever she heard of someone in trouble. Besides her volunteer work at the nearby South County Hospital and the animal rescue groups, she listened for emergency calls on an old police scanner that had belonged to her father when he'd been a volunteer fireman. Her experiences, coupled with a wary nature, tended to make her believe all activity was suspicious until proven otherwise.

"I doubt that Peg needs my help," Edna protested. "The police may already have all the answers they need. I have only initial impressions and those are probably unreliable at this point. Virginia has died, maybe from food poisoning, but maybe from another cause, since nobody else seems to have suffered." As Edna spoke the words, a shocking thought popped into her head. *Might Virginia have committed suicide?*

"I can almost hear the wheels turning, Mom. What are you thinking?"

Edna shook herself mentally as Starling's words shattered the gruesome idea. She didn't want to speculate any further until she had more information. Besides, the thought was ridiculous. "I don't want to guess," she said, avoiding a direct answer to her daughter's question. Not wanting to dwell on the awful news, she said, "What are your plans for the day?" Her gaze went from Starling to

Mary and back, inviting either or both to answer.

"I was going to drive Jaycee up the coast toward Wickford, but it doesn't look like the weather is going to cooperate."

"What about some sort of inside activity, like visiting Gilbert Stuart's birthplace," Edna suggested. "She might be interested in learning about the artist who painted the portrait used on our one-dollar bill."

"You could take her to the South County Museum." Mary chimed in. "That place is kinda fun, and they have exhibits of home cooking from over a hundred years ago. Jaycee could get some ideas for her book."

Starling wrinkled her nose in disappointment. "Nice places and good ideas, but I was hoping to be outside this week. I spend so much time in the studio." She sighed. "I'll see what Jaycee would like to do. She said she'd be over around nine this morning."

Edna glanced up at the wall clock behind her daughter. "It's nearly twenty after. Maybe she figured you wouldn't be going anywhere in this rain and decided to stay home."

Starling pushed her chair back from the table. "I didn't realize it was that late. I'll go over and knock on her door."

"She might be sleeping in this morning. She had a late visitor." Mary had a knack for dropping conversational bombshells. "I heard a motorcycle. After midnight," she added, raising an eyebrow.

The news brought to Edna's mind the

image of a dark figure standing in Jaycee's driveway about the time the storm had begun. That would have been more than an hour after Mary heard the bike, though. Edna was about to mention her sighting, but Mary leapt up in the quick way she had of leaving. Her hurried departures typically followed one of her verbal grenades.

As soon as his mistress moved, Hank was on his feet, tail wagging. "I gotta look for the kitten. Maybe Hank can find her." She ran her hand over the top of the dog's head. Looking at Edna, she said, "Call me when you find out what happened to your friend's housekeeper, okay?" Her eyes glowed with anticipation, but she didn't wait for Edna to reply, confident of an affirmative answer. "Thanks for breakfast," she called over her shoulder as she and her dog disappeared through the mudroom to the back door. Starling was already on her way to the front door and the neighbor's house across the street.

Left alone, Edna straightened up the kitchen before heading for her office to call Albert. She was reaching for the phone when she heard the front door open.

"Whew, it's nasty out there," Starling called from the hall before appearing in the doorway. Removing her rain-spattered coat, she said. "No answer to my knock. I'm sure we agreed to get together this morning. Maybe Mary's right about Jaycee sleeping in."

At that moment, Edna remembered the soggy note she'd found beneath the newspaper and, explaining to Starling, they both went back to the kitchen where the ink-stained paper had been pushed to the back of the counter.

"What do you make of this?" She handed the now-dry page to Starling. "Could this be a note for you? It must have been stuck on the door. I found it on the wet stoop under the newspaper this morning."

Starling frowned over the scrap. "The first word looks like GO- something."

"That's what I thought, too, but I couldn't make out the rest. Could it be 'going' or 'gone'?"

"You mean like 'gone fishin'?" Starling gave a short laugh at her own humor before saying more seriously. "I think the -RRY at the end might be 'sorry' and she was breaking our plans for today."

"You might be right," Edna mused.

Starling tossed the wrinkled paper back onto the counter. Half joking, since the weather had dampened her plans anyway, she said, "Well, that's a fine 'howdy do' after I planned the day to show her around. Maybe I'll call Charlie and see what he's doing. What's the forecast?"

"I haven't heard, but it looks to me like we'll have rain off and on all day." Turning her thoughts to her own plans, Edna sympathized with her daughter. "I'm sorry your plans fell through, dear, but if Peg needs me, I'll probably drive back to Providence."

Starling went upstairs to phone Charlie on her mobile, and Edna returned to her office. Deciding to phone Peg first instead of Albert, she entered the Providence number.

Peg picked up on the second ring, sounding weary. In answer to Edna's query, she said, "No, I didn't get much sleep last night. Geoff's still in bed, and Stephen's gone to the bank, work as usual." She spoke offhandedly, as if she didn't mind, but Edna resented Stephen's callousness. He should have stayed home with Peg at a time like this. Certainly, he could take time away from his precious bank for once. Peg's voice interrupted Edna's bitter thoughts.

"I was going to make breakfast, but I don't seem to have the energy. Besides, the police took away most of our food."

"Have you heard from them as to cause of death?"

"Not yet. It will take time, they said, but didn't tell me how *much* time."

"Would you like me to bring you some groceries?"

"No, thanks, Ed. Geoff should be up soon. I'll see if he wants to go out for breakfast somewhere."

"Okay, but I'll be home, so call me if you need anything."

After hanging up, she was still staring at the phone when Starling came downstairs a few minutes later. "Charlie's coming over. He said to tell you he has news about Jaycee. He sounded concerned that she didn't show up this morning or answer the door. He also didn't like the fact that she might have had a visitor in the middle of the night. Sounds to me like he's making a mountain out of a mole hill."

Edna decided Charlie must not have told Starling about the call from his friend Dietz and the request to keep an eye on Jaycee. Looking thoughtfully at the drawer that held Jaycee's envelope, she wondered if it was time to show it to Charlie.

Chapter Fourteen

While they waited for Charlie to arrive,
Edna phoned Albert. He picked up immediately,
but his voice didn't hold its usual enthusiasm.
"Hello, sweetheart."

Edna was on immediate alert. "You sound
tired, dear, or discouraged. Is Stan not doing
well?"

"He's doing as well as can be expected,
but I'm not getting much sleep. Bea wants to talk
long into the night about their wedding, his work,
their plans for his retirement. I think it's her way
of holding onto him--something like, if she keeps
talking, he won't die--but she's wearing me out."
He gave a short laugh, trying to insert some humor
into the situation.

"What's his prognosis? Is it so bad that
Bea feels she'll lose him?"

"Actually, his doctors and I are encouraged
with his progress. Bea's imagining the worst. He's
getting a couple of stents tomorrow morning. I'll
be in the O.R., but only to observe. He's not as
strong as we'd like to see, but the doctors here
don't think there's any danger with him going into
surgery. I agree with them. If he pulls through, and
I have no reason to think he won't, I'll stick
around here with Bea if we can't move him by the
end of the week."

"How are George and Arthur?" Edna asked
about the other men who made up the foursome

for the week's golfing getaway.

"They leave Sunday morning, as planned. Since it's early in the season, the manager will let me rent the condo for however long we'll need it, but I doubt it will be more than a few days before Stan's ready to travel. I'll rent a car and drive him and Bea home." Albert changed the subject abruptly. "Enough about Stan. Tell me how you are. Any big news on the home front? How are the kids?"

Not wanting to add to his worries by telling him about Virginia, Edna merely said, "Nothing new at home, dear. The children are fine. Starling is spending a few days with me, and we miss you." At that moment, a flash of lightning flooded the room with its brilliance, followed by a clap of thunder so loud that Edna nearly dropped the phone.

"What was that?" Albert shouted. "What's going on back there?"

"We're having rain and thunder. The storm seems to be getting worse, so I'm going to hang up. I'll call you later." Without bothering to wait for his reply, she disconnected. Having grown up with land lines and the danger they presented from lightning, she was still uncomfortable about using a phone during severe storms. Besides, it was hard to hear over the claps of thunder and the rain beating against the windows.

Charlie still hadn't shown up and Starling had gone up to her room to work on her computer, so Edna dusted and polished the furniture in living and dining rooms to work off some nervous energy. She thought about Peg and Virginia, and wondered where Jaycee might have gone. Edna wished the note hadn't been washed out. Had someone really been walking up Jaycee's driveway last night or had the image been a trick of light and shadow? Had Mary heard a motorcycle or had that too been a trick of the imagination? How did she know the late-night rider was visiting Jaycee and not simply passing through the neighborhood? Edna's head was beginning to ache with so many unanswered questions.

Absently, she put away the dust cloth and furniture polish and went to her office where she opened the drawer and stared at the manila envelope. She wondered again if she should show it to Charlie. They wouldn't open it, of course, but maybe he could call the number. She was fantasizing about who would answer if they were to phone Chicago when she heard the doorbell chime. Closing the drawer with a guilty start for thinking of betraying Jaycee's implied confidence, she rose to greet Charlie.

Starling sprinted down the stairs and was heading for the front door as Edna reached the hall. "I'll get it," she said, hurrying to let her detective in out of the rain.

"Hmmm," he murmured, kissing her lightly on the lips, then blushing as he raised his eyes and caught Edna's smile.

"Come in," she greeted him, swallowing a laugh at his sheepish expression. "We'll light the fire in the living room and talk there."

Starling pulled Charlie to the sofa to sit with her at right angles to the hearth. Edna sat in her favorite armchair across the coffee table from them. Leaning forward with his elbows on his knees, Charlie stared fixedly into Edna's face for several seconds before speaking.

"Have you told her anything about Dietz's call," he asked, flicking his eyes toward Starling.

"No," she responded. "Have you?"

"Hey, you two," Starling cut in. "I'm in the room. Sitting right here. You don't have to talk around me."

Charlie sat back and took her hand. "Sorry, babe. I only wanted to know where to start."

She pulled her hand away and half turned on the seat to face him. "You can start by telling me what's going on. Who's Dietz?"

So Charlie told her about the hurried phone call and about asking Edna to help him by getting to know Jaycee.

"That's the story," he concluded, reaching again for her hand. "I don't want her to know we're keeping an eye on her until I find out why Dietz wants her watched. When she told your mother about needing pictures to illustrate a cookbook, introducing the two of you seemed like the perfect solution for us to learn more about her and, at the same time, keep her under observation."

Starling crossed her arms over her chest, tucking her hands out of his reach. She glowered first at Charlie, then at Edna. "Why didn't either of you fill me in," she snapped. "I feel like you don't trust me."

"Of course we trust you, dear," Edna said soothingly before Charlie could speak and make matters worse. "We didn't want to take the chance that you would feel self-conscious and make Jaycee suspicious. If she's hiding something, she would have clammed up. If she isn't hiding anything, we could frighten her unnecessarily. We wanted you just to be yourself, get to know her and be friends."

"And then you would have pumped *me* for information. I see." Starling's face was flushed with resentment.

Edna knew the best way to defuse her daughter would be to ignore her irritation and bring her into the conspiracy. "Let's hear what Charlie has found out, and you can help us decide what to do next."

Arms still crossed tightly over her chest, Starling slouched back into her corner of the sofa and stared expectantly at the man seated next to her.

Looking none too happy himself, Charlie leaned back into his own corner and stretched out his legs, crossing his ankles beneath the coffee table.

"The woman who bought the house next door is Joanna Cravendorf, not Jaycee Watkins," he began to explain what his investigation had unearthed to date. "Cravendorf lives in Florida under the name Jo Fitzgerald. She's a widow and 'filthy rich,' as the saying goes. Gerry Fitzgerald was her fourth husband."

That bit of news made both Edna and Starling sit up with interest and curiosity. Starling unfolded her arms and brought her knees up onto the seat. Her eyes widened as she faced Charlie square on.

"And she's a relation of Jaycee's?" Starling's guess was posed as a question.

He nodded. "Her grandmother. Cravendorf's second husband was Ira James, Jaycee's grandfather. When she was married to James, Joanna went by the name of Anna. For some reason, she used a different variation of her first name with each husband."

"So where does the name Cravendorf come into it and why didn't she use her present name to buy across the street," Starling asked, now looking more curious than angry.

"First husband, deceased," Charlie said, "and the one whose legacy she used to make the purchase. I don't know why."

"Maybe because he was the one she was married to when they lived in Westerly," Edna suggested. "All these names for one person are very confusing. Can we agree to call her Joanna for the purpose of our conversation?" When Charlie nodded his consent, she continued, "Is she Jaycee's maternal or paternal grandmother? Where does the name Watkins come in?"

"Joanna is Jaycee's maternal grandmother. Actually, Ira James is still living. I traced him to a nursing home near Chicago. He's not well, but he's alive."

"Chicago." *At last, a connection*, Edna

thought, visualizing the phone number on the envelope in her desk drawer. She still was uncertain about showing it to Charlie. Would he insist on opening it? She thought he would probably see no sense in only looking at the outside of the envelope. Aloud, she said, "You've found grandparents, but where are Jaycee's parents?"

"I think they died in an automobile accident, but I'm trying to verify that."

"What about your friend Dietz? Does he know anything about the family?"

"I haven't been able to reach him. My guess is he's on a case and has left his personal cell phone at home. He carries a phone with a blocked number when he's in the field, so he won't be getting non-essential calls at inappropriate times."

While Edna and Charlie were talking, Starling had left the room and returned with her mobile on which she was typing rapidly. Distracted and slightly irritated by her daughter's rudeness, Edna was about to suggest that she go to another room if she wanted to text people when Starling suddenly flipped the phone around so they could see what she'd been doing.

"I thought Jaycee looked familiar. When you mentioned the name James, I remembered. Don't you think this is Jaycee?" She passed the phone to Charlie who examined the portrait on the tiny display before passing it across the low table to Edna.

With her artist's eye for faces, she agreed

immediately. "Her hair is longer and darker, but either this is Jaycee or she has an identical twin."

"That's a picture of Carol James," Starling informed the other two. "She's a free-lance photojournalist. I caught an article about her in a magazine a few months ago. That's where I remember seeing her picture. I *knew* she looked familiar," Starling added, puffed with pleasure at having solved a piece of the puzzle. "She was featured in an online article after she got some incredible pictures of an arsonist setting fire to someone's house. It was a suburb of Chicago, and thank goodness the family got out okay. According to the article, Carol James caught the arsonist purely by accident. She was in the ritzy neighborhood taking pictures for a photo spread in which she intended to compare the wealth of residents to the elaborateness of their Christmas decorations. Apparently, the guy intended to make the fire look like it had been caused by faulty wiring in a string of lights."

Edna thought the story was interesting, but she noticed that Charlie was listening with rapt attention. "I think it's about time I paid a visit to your neighbor." He pushed himself up from the sofa.

"She's not home," Starling said, and told him how she'd gone to Jaycee's earlier that morning.

He shook his head in a stubborn gesture. "She might be back by now. I'm going to check."

"Then I'll come with you." Starling stood, an angry note in her voice. "If she *is* home, I want to know why she pretended not to know a thing about photography. I feel like a fool, giving kiddy lessons to an award-winning photojournalist." She looked at Edna. "You coming, Mom?"

"I don't think so, dear. I'd like to hear what she has to say, but I think I'll stay here in case Peg should call." Thinking of her friend, Edna put up a hand to stop Charlie from leaving the room. "Have you found out anything about Goran Pittlani?"

"Only that he has a strange name. 'Goran' is a popular Slavic name and 'Pittlani' is Taiwanese. Quite a combination," he said before following Starling into the front hall.

Impatient with having to wait for news, Edna wondered what she should do to occupy herself and keep from going stir crazy. Her primary choice for relaxation was to putter in the garden. Obviously, she wouldn't be doing that today. Cooking was a second-best activity, so she went to the pantry in the mudroom for her recipe card file and brought it to the kitchen table. She had browsed about a third of the cards in the file, having found nothing to tempt her so far, when she heard the side door open and then close quickly again to shut out the noise of the storm. She was about to rise when she heard Charlie and Starling talking and guessed they'd come in through the mudroom to avoid dripping water over the front hall rugs and wood floor.

"That didn't take long," she greeted them as they entered the kitchen.

"She's still not home." Looking dejected,

Starling slid onto one of the kitchen chairs. When Benjamin jumped into her lap, she mechanically began to stroke his fur. "I think you're right about the note. She must have written to cancel our plans for today."

"Do you know what vehicles she owns?" Charlie asked Edna, lowering himself onto the chair next to Starling's.

"What do you mean?"

Her daughter replied. "When she didn't answer the door, we looked in the garage windows to see if her car was there. Her car is gone, but there's a motorcycle parked next to her scooter." She frowned. "It seems like an awfully big bike for Jaycee, and why would she have both a motorcycle and a scooter?"

Edna thought for a few seconds and frowned. "The only motorcycle I've seen around here belongs to Peg's gardener."

"A gardener who rides a Harley," Starling said with amazement. Before Edna could respond, Starling turned to Charlie with a sudden twinkle in her eye. "There are depths to Mom and her friends that I will probably never know."

Edna smiled to acknowledge her daughter's teasing, but she didn't feel cheered or pleased. She repeated with emphasis for Charlie's benefit. "Except for the occasional scooter like the one Jaycee has, Goran's is the only motorized bike I've seen in the neighborhood since we moved in last year."

Starling looked skeptical. "What would Aunt Peg's gardener's bike be doing in Jaycee's garage?"

"That's what I'd like to know, but I can't think of anyone else it might belong to," Edna replied. She puzzled over the implications before explaining to the others. "They know each other, so it's possible it's Goran's bike, but I introduced them only yesterday afternoon when Jaycee stopped by to give me your message." She spoke to Starling before turning to Charlie. "Peg sent Goran to pick up some iris bulbs. Jaycee was here when he arrived, so I invited the two of them in to tea." She stopped to imagine her two guests in the kitchen, wondering if she'd missed some spark between them. Deciding she hadn't, she went on, "I had hoped to learn something about either one, but they both were extremely adroit at dodging personal questions."

Charlie frowned. "It sure looks like they've gone off together. Are you certain they'd never met before yesterday?"

"Maybe Goran's a fast mover," Starling interjected, gently poking Charlie in the ribs with her elbow.

The disquiet Edna had felt in Goran's presence came flooding back into the pit of her stomach. "What if Jaycee didn't go off with him willingly?"

"What do you mean? You think she was kidnapped?" Starling's tone implied how absurd she thought the idea. "What would give you an idea like that?"

"I don't know," Edna replied hesitantly. "Something has been bothering me about Goran since I first met him. Whenever I've been around him, I've had the feeling that he's not who he pretends to be."

"Look," Charlie interrupted the conversation between mother and daughter. "We've nothing to go on except the fact that her car is gone and his motorcycle, if it *is* his, is in her garage. Other than the fact that they've driven off somewhere, probably together, there is no reason to suspect foul play." He ran a hand through his hair and stood up. "I've got to get back to work. Call me if you hear from her, okay?"

"We will," Edna said as he turned toward the mudroom to retrieve his coat. "And you'll let me know if you find out anything about Goran?"

She thought again of the envelope lying in her desk drawer, but as before, decided to say nothing about it. If Jaycee didn't show up by the end of the day, she might think more seriously about showing it to Charlie, but for now, he was right. There was no reason to suspect anything sinister had occurred.

Chapter Fifteen

"What will you do today?" Edna asked Starling when Charlie had gone. The question was mostly for conversation and to distract herself from the myriad of unsettling thoughts galloping around in her head.

"If the rain ever lets up, I might drive along the coast and photograph the waves. I'd love to get some decent shots of spindrift, but that depends on the wind, of course." Walking to the sink, she looked out the window and sighed. "It doesn't look like it will clear any time soon. I guess I'll go upstairs and work on my laptop for a while." She turned quickly to face Edna. "I wasn't thinking, Mom. If you're going to drive to Aunt Peg's, would you like me to go with you?"

"No, dear. Thanks, but I'm not certain Peg will even want me to visit. Geoff was still there when I spoke to her this morning, so she's not alone. I'll read for a bit and, if I don't hear from her first, I'll call her later to see how she's doing."

Edna put a disc of Chopin piano music on the player in the living room and had just settled in her chair by the still glowing fire with her knitting when the phone rang. It was Peg.

"How are you feeling," Edna asked.

"I'm better, thanks." Peg sounded only slightly less tired than she had earlier.

"Is Geoff with you?"

"He left a few minutes ago."

"Would you like company? I could drive up."

"You're a true blue friend, Ed. What would I do without you?" Peg paused briefly, as if to consider Edna's offer, then said, "If you don't mind the drive to Providence again, I'd love your company. I want to start organizing Virginia's belongings, but I don't relish the thought of going through her rooms by myself. I spoke with her sister this morning. Janette lives in New Hampshire. She and her husband will drive down as soon as we know when the body will be released, and we'll talk about funeral arrangements then, too."

"Did she have relatives other than her sister?"

"A nephew and a niece and three or four cousins, I think. Janette is going to notify the rest of the family."

"Do you need boxes for Virginia's belongings? I think we still have a stack out in the garage left over from our move last year."

"That would be nice. I'm sure I'll need them. We can only guess at what Janette will want to keep and what she'll want to give away, so we'll have to organize and label carefully--which means lots of boxes." Peg sounded as if she were getting tired just talking about what needed to be done. "When can you get here?"

"I'll leave at once and should be there in less than an hour." After ending the call, Edna went upstairs to let Starling know she was leaving.

"I'll call if I won't be home for supper,"

she told her daughter.

"And I'll call *you* if I get Charlie to take me to dinner. He owes me a few evenings for all the dates he's cancelled." Starling gave a crooked smile. "I'm not holding my breath, though. Two nights off in a row is rare for that guy." More somberly, she added, "Give my love to Aunt Peg and tell her I'm so sorry about Virginia."

Edna nodded, hugged her child and headed to Providence for the third time that week. She was grateful to notice the rain and wind lessening as she drove farther north. She made good time and was at Peg's doorstep in forty-five minutes.

Looking pale and drawn, Peg let Edna into the house and, after a long hug, the two friends went through to the kitchen.

"I made tea," Peg said, placing both hands on the kitchen table and lowering herself onto a chair. She had dark circles beneath her eyes, and her brow was creased with concern.

Edna was alarmed, sensing something besides grief in her friend. Removing the cozy from the tea pot, she sat and began to pour as she waited for Peg to speak.

"The police called about twenty minutes ago," Peg began, staring at the stream of hot liquid cascading into her cup. "They said Virginia was poisoned."

Edna frowned, confused. "That's what you've thought all along, isn't it? Food poisoning?"

"Apparently what they found is not typical food poisoning. The medical examiner discovered a toxin in her blood that's similar to snake venom."

"Snake venom?" Edna was skeptical. "Where would snake venom have come from? There aren't any poisonous snakes native to Rhode Island. When could she have been bitten, and wouldn't she have said something to you?" Edna shuddered at the thought of snake bites and considered the garden. Maybe Goran had stirred up a nest with all the tilling he'd been doing.

Peg broke into her thoughts. "It wasn't an actual snake bite. The poison is something that acts in the body *like* snake venom, they said."

"What exactly does that mean?"

Peg shook her head. "They didn't go into detail, only told me not to touch anything in her rooms. The police are sending a forensic team to go through everything." She pulled a handkerchief from the pocket of her slacks and began to dab at the tears welling in her eyes. "I don't understand any of this. How could Virginia have been poisoned, and in this house?"

Edna reached across the table to put her hand on Peg's arm. "Have you eaten today?"

Peg shook her head before blowing her nose. "I don't think I could hold anything down."

"What about soup? Shall I heat some for you?"

Peg shrugged and gave Edna a weak smile. "I know you're right. Maybe a little soup will be good. Thanks, Ed."

Opening the pantry door, she noticed an apron hanging on the back. Plucking it off the

hook, she draped it over her head and tugged on
the sash to tie it behind her waist. As she did so,
she felt something hard bump against her thigh.
Reaching into the pocket, she pulled out Virginia's
red rosary. It was made of seeds, Edna realized,
and not ceramic as she had supposed when she'd
seen it in Virginia's hands a few days before. Each
scarlet seed had a jet-black spot on one end. She
turned toward Peg, studying the strand as
something began to nag at her subconscious, but
before she could bring the thought into focus,
Peg's question distracted her.

"What have you found?"

"Something you'll want to put with
Virginia's things," Edna answered, striding to the
table, her hand outstretched with the rosary
dangling from her fingers.

Peg was reaching for the rosary when a
faint noise caused her to look behind Edna, and
her eyes widened with surprise. Edna swung
around to see Stephen standing in the doorway to
the dining room. In three long strides, he crossed
to her and took the rosary before she could either
move or object.

"We're seeing a lot of you lately," he said,
gazing briefly at the red necklace, as if it held little
interest. Switching his gaze to Edna, he slipped the
rosary into his coat pocket before moving to the
coffee pot on the counter beside the stove. Neither
woman spoke as they watched him take a mug
from the cupboard above the machine and pour
himself some coffee. He then turned and rested a
hip against the oven door. Arms crossed and mug

balanced in the crook of his elbow, he stared at Edna as if waiting for an explanation of her presence. His expression was placid, the rosary apparently forgotten.

Before Edna could recover her astonishment at Stephen's arrogance, Peg spoke. "What are you doing home, Stephen? I thought you had a meeting."

"The police called. Said they would be going through Virginia's things, so I rearranged my schedule. I don't want you to have to deal with them." His eyes flicked to Peg before returning to Edna. It was as if he were willing her to disappear, as if silently telling her she wasn't needed now that he was home.

She stood her ground. "I was about to heat some soup for lunch. Would you like to join us?" She knew she was being impertinent since, technically, it was his home, but she had never thought of the house as belonging to anyone but Peg's family. It was the Graystocking Mansion, as far as she was concerned. Always was, always would be.

In the middle of an awkwardly growing silence, the doorbell rang. Stephen dropped his eyes, set his coffee cup on the counter and strode from the kitchen to answer the door. Edna knew it would be the police and was surprised that, instead of leading them through the kitchen, which would have been the usual way to reach Virginia's rooms, he took them up the front stairs. The two women looked at each other and then at the ceiling, following the sound of heavy footsteps that mounted the three wooden steps leading to what had been servants quarters when the house had been built in the late nineteenth century.

Edna turned to Peg. "Why would Stephen take Virginia's rosary?"

Peg shrugged and seemed resigned. "I don't know. Maybe he wants to be the one to give it to the police."

Deciding not to press the subject, Edna resumed her chore, mixing together and heating a can each of potato and cheddar cheese soups. She put out a plate of saltines, and, as the two friends ate lunch, Peg talked about the early days when Virginia had first come to work for the Graystockings. Each time her quiet chatter was broken by a muffled noise from above, she winced.

Edna murmured an occasional encouragement during the meal, sensing that Peg needed to talk, but her curiosity had been aroused. At the first opportunity, once they had cleared the table and Peg fell silent, Edna said, "Tell me about the lunch yesterday. Did things go well with the Froissards?"

"Sort of." Some color had returned to Peg's face and she seemed to have perked up a little after eating. Frowning slightly, she took a minute before explaining. "I think Renee was angry with Virginia, although she tried to hide her feelings."

"What do you mean? Did they quarrel?"

"Not exactly. It's hard to put my finger on." Peg hesitated and drifted off in thought for a minute. "I sensed that Renee wanted something from Virginia, but Virginia was ignoring her. She could be very stubborn."

"If it wasn't obvious, what makes you think there was anything wrong?"

Peg shrugged. "There was a tension between them. Renee seemed to be trying to say something to Virginia--kind of a silent communication--but Virginia wouldn't look at her. Mostly, it was the body language between the two that made me uncomfortable."

"Did Guy notice it, too?"

"I think so, but I can't be certain." Peg shrugged. "Maybe it's my imagination and they were just uncomfortable being back in the house after so long and all that happened." Her brow creased with thought and she stared at her fingers as they shredded a tissue in her lap. "Renee and Guy arrived shortly before noon. Virginia and I greeted them at the door. Then Virginia went back to the kitchen to finish making lunch while I showed the Froissards around downstairs. I wanted them to see that I haven't changed the place very much. After the short tour, I took them into the living room and asked if they'd like some cider before lunch. Renee said she'd get it because she'd like a word with Virginia."

"Did she seem angry at that time?"

Peg thought about the question before slowly shaking her head. "I'd say she seemed more edgy or maybe annoyed rather than angry."

Edna didn't think the description sounded like someone intent on murder. "What about Guy?

Did he also seem as if he were irritated with Virginia?"

In answering, Peg continued to walk Edna through the events of the afternoon. "When Renee returned with glasses of cider, she motioned for her brother to go to the kitchen. It was just a small jerk of her head. I caught it out of the corner of my eye, and I don't think she realized I'd seen her. I was telling him about my plans for the yard, and we were going over the old photographs when she walked in."

"So he went to the kitchen?"

"Yes. He took the tray from Renee and set it on the coffee table, then said she'd forgotten napkins. I said I'd get them, but he said to never mind, he was already up. Renee might have purposely forgotten napkins so Guy would have an excuse to talk to Virginia."

"So they were both in the kitchen while Virginia was preparing lunch, but at different times." Edna spoke the thought almost to herself before asking. "Was anyone else in the kitchen with her?"

Peg nodded. "I was. I helped with the salad. Goran came in for his lunch while Virginia and I were getting things ready. He finished eating about the time the Froissards arrived, when we went to answer the door."

Edna grimaced. "Seems like the kitchen was a busy place yesterday."

Peg concurred. "Stephen was here, too. Remember? The Froissards and I were in the living room when he walked in, and I'm embarrassed to say my husband didn't hide his displeasure over my having company."

"I remember you telling me he'd come home unexpectedly. Hadn't you told him about having guests for lunch?"

"Of course I had, but he acted as if their presence were totally unexpected."

"Do you suppose his surprise was just an act and he came home purposely? Maybe he was curious about old friends of yours." *Or jealous, he's so possessive of you.* Edna did not speak this last thought aloud.

Peg shrugged. "I've given up trying to guess what motivates him. I made the introductions, and he left to let Virginia know he'd be joining us for lunch. That was the big surprise, that he wanted to stay. You know how uncomfortable he is with strangers."

Edna thought "uncomfortable" was a diplomatic way of describing Stephen's aloofness at social events, but she kept silent. Instead, she said, "So at one time or another, everyone had been in the kitchen alone or with only Virginia when the food was being prepared."

"I'm afraid so, but I can't think why any one of us would want to harm Virginia. It's absurd, some sort of horrible mistake."

Edna knew thinking that way was futile. The fact was Virginia was dead, and she'd been poisoned. Edna began to wonder how long Goran had been alone in the kitchen and if she'd get a chance to ask him. Aloud, she said, "What was served for lunch?"

"Virginia did her usual brilliant job," Peg's eyes moistened with memory and remorse. "The plates were attractive and colorful. She made baked chicken breasts with homemade cranberry relish and a salad ... a slaw really, with shredded cabbage and carrots, chopped radishes and walnuts. And she baked cherry cobbler for dessert. One of my favorites." The tissue in her lap having been torn to bits, Peg reached for a paper napkin in the holder on the table to dab at her sudden tears.

"So each plate was indistinguishable from the others." Edna spoke almost to herself as she wondered what was the possibility Virginia had not been the target.

"Almost," Peg said. "Virginia's wouldn't have had walnuts. She was allergic. They gave her hives."

Edna briefly bent her head to mull over what she had learned about the previous afternoon's activities. When she looked up again, she noticed her friend's tears flowing in earnest and was about to distract Peg by asking after Cherisse when footsteps sounded on the back stairs.

Virginia's rooms were above the kitchen and consisted of a bedroom and a sitting room with a full bathroom between. When the house had first been built, all three rooms had been servants' sleeping quarters. Peg's father hired a contractor to convert the middle room into a bathroom when the family reduced the number of live-in staff. The bathroom, in fact, had been a necessity when maids no longer put up with outdoor facilities or bathing in cold water.

Stairs descended from the bedroom to a narrow mudroom with access to both the yard and the kitchen. A small lavatory had been added off the room, opposite the back stairs, for the convenience of household and yard workers.

At the moment, Stephen entered the kitchen from this back entryway, followed by another man. Peg looked at her husband expectantly, but it was the stranger who introduced himself as Detective Ian Ruthers. He was about six feet tall, dressed in black slacks and a herringbone sports coat over a crisply ironed pearl-gray shirt. His maroon tie was plain and neatly knotted. Edna guessed him to be in his mid-fifties and liked the soft baritone of his voice.

"We're almost finished upstairs, Mrs. Bishop. I understand our team went through the kitchen last night, so we'll just have a quick look around and be on our way." He glanced at Stephen before turning back to Peg. His words were for them both. "I must ask you to keep yourselves available for the next few days. We may have questions, once the lab work has been completed."

"Of course," Peg answered quietly.

Nodding his assent to Detective Ruthers, Stephen motioned with an upturned palm for the man to precede him into the dining room.

Before they could disappear, Edna surprised everyone in the room by blurting, "Stephen, did you remember to give Virginia's rosary to the police?"

For the flash of an instant, his narrowed eyes held hatred so raw that Edna's breath caught in her throat. Because of the way they were standing, nobody else would have seen the look and she herself wondered if it had been a trick of the light, the spark faded so quickly. His face looked both innocent and startled when he turned to face the detective.

"I'd completely forgotten." He sounded sincere as he pulled the beads from his pocket. "I don't think an old rosary could be very important." Holding the scarlet necklace with its silver cross up to the detective, he said, "Do you want it?"

"Everything's important at this point, sir." Detective Ruthers took a small paper bag from the inside pocket of his jacket and held it open to receive the offering. After closing the little sack, he tucked it into a side pocket while he looked curiously at Stephen. Ignoring the look, Stephen turned and led the way out of the room.

In the silence that followed their exit, Edna wondered if the rosary really had slipped Stephen's mind, before mentally chiding herself. Was her imagination working overtime? Why would he want to hide a string of prayer beads from the police?

Chapter Sixteen

Two hours later, Edna was sitting in a rocking chair beside the brick fireplace in Peg's library. She was re-reading Louisa May Alcott's "Little Women" she'd found in one of the built-in bookshelves. Peg was asleep on a sofa facing the same hearth across an antique cobbler's bench that served as a coffee table. She was huddled beneath a hand-knitted green and gold afghan, her snores so soft as to be barely audible. The fire had not been lighted, the room being warm enough. Edna was feeling drowsy and her eye lids were beginning to droop when the doorbell rang.

Peg woke with a start. "Whaaa ..." she mumbled, looking around as if trying to figure out where she was.

"Stay put," Edna said, getting to her feet. "I'll go."

She opened the door to Detective Ruthers and, when he asked for Mrs. Bishop, Edna showed him to the library. Peg was sitting up by the time they entered the room. She'd folded the afghan and draped it over the back of the couch. She didn't rise at the detective's greeting, but motioned him to the overstuffed chair opposite Edna's rocker.

"We found the source of the poison," he said, once they were seated and he'd refused the offer of tea or coffee. "The beads of your housekeeper's rosary are known as lucky beans or rosary peas. According to the lab techs, they are very toxic, and apparently, Ms. Hoxie ate one."

Peg gasped, raising a hand to her mouth. Edna nodded, a thought that had been hovering at the back of her mind jarred loose by the news. "I read about rosary peas in Mrs. Rabichek's journals," she said, referring to the notebooks that her house's former owner had left to her. "The poison is abrin, as I recall." She frowned. "But symptoms don't usually show up for a day or more. Are you saying she was poisoned prior to yesterday?"

"Partially true," he said. "The medical examiner thinks some of the poison had already been absorbed through her skin by her fingering the beads. The outer shell usually protects against that, but holes drilled to allow the seeds to be strung together plus the constant rubbing eroded the shell, exposing her to the poison."

"Could enough poison be absorbed that way to cause so sudden a reaction," Edna asked, still dubious. "Wouldn't she have had symptoms before yesterday?"

The detective raised his eyebrows at Edna. "You know a lot about this poison."

She didn't know if he expected an answer or not, so she kept quiet.

Several seconds passed during which he studied her face before he turned back to Peg. "The M.E. says enough of this abrin had gotten into her system through her skin that when she ate a whole seed, the effects created a severe enough reaction to bring on her heart attack." He kept his eyes on Peg's when he said, "I assume you knew she had a weak heart."

Peg nodded. "She had rheumatic fever as a child."

"We're continuing our investigation, but we haven't entirely ruled out the possibility that it may have been suicide."

"No," Peg gasped, jerking herself up to glare at Ruthers. "You are mistaken. Virginia would *never* have taken her own life. She was a devout Catholic." Frowning, she added, "Besides which she had no reason to take her own life."

"Mrs. Bishop," the detective said patiently, "we're pretty sure a seed was deliberately cut from the necklace, so either she did it herself or someone else did."

"Breaking the shell made the poison lethal because of her heart condition," Edna said. She hadn't meant to speak aloud, but she couldn't hold back the dreadful thought.

"Exactly," Ruthers said, flicking a glance in her direction, but he seemed alert to every nuance in Peg's face. "The findings of the autopsy are unmistakable. The seed was cut. It did not accidentally fall into Ms. Hoxie's food." He fidgeted with a set of car keys in his fingers, finally looking away from the shock and denial on Peg's face.

She turned incredulous eyes to Edna who gave a short shake of her head and a slight nod in Ruthers's direction. She hoped Peg would get the message that any objection or further discussion would do no good. Apparently, she did get the message, because she stood abruptly and held out a hand to the detective.

"Thank you for coming to tell me," she said simply. "What do you require from us?"

He pushed himself up from the chair and briefly took her hand. "I'd like you and your husband to come down to the station this afternoon and make formal statements as to what occurred here yesterday. We'll be talking to everyone involved. We'll also need to know which funeral home you'll be using so we can have the body sent over to them."

"I'll let you know after I've spoken with her sister," Peg responded, seeming to drift away into stunned disbelief. When she sank back onto the sofa and covered her face with her hands, Edna showed Ruthers to the front door and shook his hand in farewell, thanking him again for his consideration in breaking the news personally. From the weary look in his eyes, she suspected notifying grieving family and friends was hard on the detective. She liked him the better for it.

Returning to the library, she sat on the sofa next to Peg and put an arm around her friend's shoulders in a brief hug.

"I don't believe it." Peg straightened up and turned toward Edna, her face suffused with anger. "It has to have been an accident. Virginia would never have done such a thing and I can't believe that anyone who was here yesterday could either."

Edna nodded absently, thinking for a minute. "Before Stephen took it out of my hand, I noticed a missing bead in one of the decades of the rosary. It slipped my mind until Detective Ruthers mentioned one had been cut from the string." She glanced at Peg. "I saw the rosary on the kitchen table more than once, just this past week. Anyone in the kitchen would have had access to it."

"Certainly we all knew about the rosary and that Virginia left it lying around at times, but who would want to harm her? Who would even know the beads were poisonous?" Peg stood determinedly. "I don't want to sit here speculating. I can't believe that someone in my house yesterday would have cause to murder Virginia, and I *will* not believe it was suicide." Without pausing for breath, she changed the subject. "If you brought boxes with you, I think I'll go up and begin sorting and packing Virginia's clothes. That's one thing I can do without consulting her sister. Do you want to help?"

"Of course," Edna said, shaking herself out of thoughts that were beginning to turn in a direction she didn't want to consider either. She'd deal with her newly-formed ideas later.

The two women brought in the boxes from Edna's car and carried them upstairs. On the way to Virginia's rooms, Peg stopped in her second-floor office to grab masking tape and markers. They dropped the collapsed cardboard in a pile in the suite's sitting room.

It was the first time Edna had been in this part of the house. She looked around with interest, noticing a number of framed photos surrounding a jade plant on a table beneath the sole window which overlooked the backyard. Moving to the table, she picked up what looked to be a fairly recent picture of Virginia. Two women, arms around each others' waists were standing behind a wheelchair on which sat an older woman. Edna recognized Renee and Cherisse as the other women in the photo.

"When was this taken?" She held the frame out to Peg.

Taking it, Peg held it to catch light from the window before handing it back. "Must have been when she visited the Froissards in Florida two or three years ago."

"Odd," Edna said, almost to herself as she looked closer at the photo.

"What's odd?" Peg had begun to assemble one of the boxes.

"Renee is wearing a red rosary that looks exactly like Virginia's."

Peg stopped what she was doing to examine the picture again. "That's right. Virginia came back from that trip with the rosary. Maybe they both have one. Oh, look, Cherisse is holding a jade plant. Do you suppose it's this same one." Peg indicated the bonsai on the table. "This picture was probably taken the day Virginia flew home. The plant and rosary might have been gifts from the Froissards."

Edna set the frame back on the table and looked at several other photos. One was of Virginia sitting beside a woman who was most likely her sister Janette. Another picture Edna thought must be Janette with her husband. A group shot, she figured to be Janette's children and grandchildren.

"Are you going to help or snoop?" Peg spoke with a touch of humor, breaking into Edna's mental wanderings. Smiling, she set the family picture back on the table and joined Peg at her task.

They constructed two boxes each and carried them through the bathroom into the bedroom. Most of Virginia's clothes hung in a long, narrow closet behind sliding doors that made up most of one bedroom wall. A chest of drawers sat opposite, and above it hung a large rectangular mirror framed in the same maple finish as the dresser.

Peg went to the closet and slid back the right-hand panel to reveal a neat row of blouses and everyday work dresses. "Let's start with these." She removed several dresses along with the hangers and turned to lay them on the bed. "I want to pack similar things together. This box will be for blouses and shirts," she announced, setting a box on the floor between them.

"Good idea," Edna agreed. "Why don't you sort things out on the bed and I'll fold and pack."

They worked companionably, speaking mainly to ask an opinion as to "which box" when Peg found a Christmas skirt of green velveteen and "should we make a rag pile" when Edna discovered a shirt with two buttons missing.

After nearly an hour, the closet was almost empty. Peg had gone to the sitting room to fetch another box when Edna reached for a red and green plaid blazer. As she slid it off its hanger, the left lapel fell forward, weighted by something pinned to the underside. She had removed it and was studying it in the palm of her hand when Peg came back into the room.

"Wha'cha got there?"

"Isn't this your mother's brooch? The one I found in the garden the other day?"

"It certainly is." Peg frowned. "Where did you get it?"

Edna showed her the jacket and explained how the brooch had been pinned beneath the lapel.

Peg was stunned. "I put it away in my room. How could it have gotten onto Virginia's jacket?"

Edna turned the pin over to examine the back. "Did you have it repaired?"

"No. Haven't had time. I stuffed it under the bras in my lingerie drawer." Peg looked sheepish. "It's one place I'm pretty sure Stephen would never think to look."

Edna couldn't help chuckling at her friend's confession, but she sobered quickly. "The brooch I found in the garden had a bent clasp. Remember? That's why we thought it had fallen off your mother's blouse and been lost in the rose garden."

"You're right." Peg's brow creased in confusion. "Maybe Virginia had it repaired, but I can't imagine her rummaging through my things. I'll go check my drawer."

Returning moments later, she displayed a

circular pin of diamonds, sapphires and rubies in her open palm. "You were right about the backing. This one's damaged. But *two* pins, exactly alike? What's going on?"

She placed her hand next to Edna's. In each woman's palm lay an identical brooch. They looked at each other in stunned silence before Edna pushed aside some clothes and sat on the bed.

Peg picked up the plaid jacket and slumped down beside Edna, folding the blazer on her lap. "What are you thinking?"

Edna said nothing for a moment as she turned the brooch over and over in her hand, lost in thought. Her gaze moved to the pin that Peg held. "One of these must be a copy, but where did it come from?"

"You mean, who made it?"

Edna nodded. "And when?"

"And how did it come to be in Virginia's closet?" Peg added as she considered the jacket on her lap. "This blazer is pretty old. Do you suppose Virginia stole Mother's brooch all those years ago and had a copy made?"

"I doubt she would have had that kind of money. A good copy would be expensive," Edna said. "Besides, why would she have it copied and then hide it away?"

"But who ..." Peg didn't have a chance to finish her sentence before Edna interrupted.

"I think we should take these and pay a visit to Cherisse. She's the only one who might be able to shed some light on this mystery."

"Do you think it was she who had a copy made?"

Edna shook her head. "She wouldn't have had that kind of money either, from what you've told me. If she had, she wouldn't have needed to work as a maid. And, again, if she had a duplicate, why wouldn't she have come forward with the copy and save herself from disgrace?"

"Let's go." Peg stood and headed for the back stairs.

Chapter Seventeen

At the nursing home, Peg knocked softly on the half-opened door to Cherisse Froissard's room before slowly pushing her way in. Edna followed to see Renee sitting next to her mother's bed with a book in her lap. It looked like a Bible. As Edna moved farther into the room, she saw Guy seated on the opposite side of the bed, holding his mother's hand. Cherisse lay propped on two pillows. She seemed to be asleep, but her eyes opened when Peg and Edna entered. She looked at them vaguely until recognition sparked some life into her face. Her lips moved as if she were about to greet them when Guy rose abruptly. Renee, sitting sideways to the door, turned her face to the wall, but not before Edna noticed her eyes were red and puffy from crying.

Edna wondered with sudden panic if Cherisse were dying. Had she and Peg stumbled into an awkward moment?

"Ladies," Guy's voice distracted Edna's attention from Cherisse as he moved toward them with arms held away from his sides, herding them back toward the open door. "Mama is not receiving visitors this afternoon. Please." He nodded toward the hall and followed them from the room, pulling the door shut behind him. "Come back another day. Today, she is tired, and my sister is not well."

"We have to talk to Cherisse," Peg said. She would have moved around him, but he placed a hand on the door frame above the strikeplate. She would have to physically push him aside to reenter the room.

"Talk to me. Maybe I can help," he said, not moving. His expression was not unfriendly, but neither was it welcoming.

Peg opened her palm to display the brooch she'd been holding in hopes of showing it to Cherisse. Edna pulled the other from her coat pocket and did the same, putting her hand beside Peg's so Guy could see them both.

"What ..." He broke off and looked from one face to the other, a quizzical expression on his face. He lowered his gaze to stare at the pins and seemed genuinely confused. "What sort of game are you playing?" His eyes sparked with anger, but strangely, his words held no conviction.

Curious but hoping to assure him, Edna spoke. "This is no game. We were hoping your mother might be able to explain the presence of two identical brooches."

"I wouldn't think so. What could she know about such a thing?" he said, staring at their hands. He brushed his own hand along the side of his head, smoothing his already neat, short-cropped gray hair.

Before he could say more, the door opened a crack and Renee looked out at her brother. Seeing her more closely, Edna thought Renee's eyes looked haunted.

"What is it, Guy? What's taking so long? Mama is calling for you."

"It's all right. Tell her I'll be in soon."

Without another word and having looked at neither Peg nor Edna, Renee stepped back and quietly closed the door.

"Let's go to the visitors lounge for a minute," Guy suggested, directing them with an open palm. "It's usually empty. We'll be private there."

The small space was actually a sunny alcove off the main corridor with several chairs positioned near wide windows that overlooked the manicured lawn two stories below. Afternoon sun warmed the room. Edna and Peg sat on a red vinyl settee that had no arms. Guy chose a wooden straight-backed chair. Seated sideways to them, he leaned forward, resting his elbows on his knees, and stared at his folded hands for several seconds before speaking. As his words came, he sat up, as if they strengthened his spine.

"We ..." he began, then gave a short cough and started again, turning to look into Peg's eyes. "Renee and I didn't know Mama had stolen your mother's brooch until this week, after your visit. When you'd left, she kept repeating over and over, 'It can't be. It can't be.' She sent Renee home to find her satin jewelry case." He squirmed on the chair as if trying to get comfortable on the hard surface. "When we gave her the case, her hands were trembling so badly, I had to help her with the zipper. I finally managed to get it open even while she kept pawing at it. I've never seen her so frantic."

He paused, not looking at Peg or Edna, but staring at his hands resting on his knees. After what seemed a very long minute, Edna was about to prod him to continue with his story when he sighed and raised his eyes to Peg. They held deep sadness. "Mama doesn't have much expensive jewelry. What she does have has been in our family for generations, except for a pearl necklace Papa gave her on their wedding day. She dumped those heirlooms out on the bed as if they were costume junk and fumbled with the padded lining at the bottom of the cloth case. At one end, concealed in the seam, there's an opening to a little compartment, a false bottom." He looked at Peg earnestly now, holding his hands palms up as if pleading. "Believe me when I tell you that Renee and I were both stunned when Mama drew out your mother's brooch. When you showed up with the one you had, she thought we'd found it and given it back to you." He shook his head as if to clear an unpleasant image. "Did your father have another made? Is that what you showed us the other day?"

"No. I would have known if Father had replaced the pin. Mother certainly would have worn it. I don't know where a copy might have come from. Edna found one circlet in the dirt along the front fence in what used to be Mother's rose garden." Peg frowned at Guy with more disbelief than anger. "So Cherisse took Mother's brooch after all," she said quietly.

"Yes," Guy nodded. Edna expected him to

hang his head in a stereotypical picture of shame. Instead, the spark of anger he'd shown earlier flashed in his eyes. "And we think, after what she suffered for it, that she should be allowed to keep the darn thing. She lost her job. Without a reference from Mrs. Graystocking, she was never again able to get work that paid a decent wage. Why she thought a few precious stones was worth all that, I don't understand, but she did and she's paid dearly for the last fifty years."

Edna was not only surprised at his reaction, but also puzzled. "If one of these is the brooch your mother took, how did it come to be pinned to a jacket in Virginia's closet? Don't tell me there's a third."

He shook his head, almost smiling at her suggestion. "We made the mistake of showing the one of Mama's to Virginia when she came to visit that evening. She asked to hold it and then wouldn't give it back. Said it belonged to you." He gestured to Peg. "We argued, and Renee even tried to grab it from her, but Virginia refused to let go. She was very stubborn and adamant about returning it to you."

"Did you try to help your sister take it back," Peg asked.

"I don't manhandle women," he said, clearly offended. "Virginia was strong. I wasn't going to fight with her."

Peg shook her head, obviously confused. "Why didn't she show it to me? Why hide it on an old jacket?"

He shrugged. "Who can say? Clearly, she

wanted to think about it or she would have given it to you at once. Virginia has been our friend for a long time. The disagreement disturbed us very much. I'm sure Virginia was unhappy about it, too."

"So that was what caused the tension between Virginia and your sister yesterday," Edna said, as the story Peg had relayed began to make more sense.

Guy nodded. "My sister got nowhere. Virginia wouldn't discuss it. I tried to reason with her also, but she was very protective of you, Peggy. I finally gave up, decided there was nothing more I could do."

He stared at Peg as if willing her to give him the answer he sought, but she dropped her eyes to study the pin she held between her fingers, turning it over and over.

Guy prodded quietly. "Will you let Mama keep her jewel? She paid dearly to possess this thing she was so infatuated with. You see, her brother had just died and she was very homesick for the old country. That pin of red, white and blue reminded her of our French flag." As if the reason weren't persuasive enough, he added even more quietly, "She won't live much longer, you know. I promise we'll give it back to you when she's gone."

Before Peg could speak and commit herself to any form of action, Edna spoke, remembering Cherisse's reaction when she'd seen the brooch in Peg's hand. "If your mother was so certain that Peg had the original brooch, she couldn't have known about a copy."

"That's right." Guy agreed and flicked his eyes to her before returning to study Peg's lowered head. He looked as if he were trying mentally to will her into submission. When she didn't respond or look up, he pressed. "What do you say, Peggy? Can she have it back, just for now?"

Impatiently, Edna shook her head, reached over and took the brooch with its bent backing from Peg's fingers. She thrust them both into her pocket as she looked from Peg to Guy. "The police need to know about these. They may not have anything to do with Virginia's death, but that's for them to decide, not us. Once this tragedy has been cleared up, you and Peg can work out who's to keep what." With that, she rose from the settee and said, "Let's go, Peg."

"Can I see Cherisse before we leave," Peg asked as she and Guy stood simultaneously.

He shook his head. "She's distressed and needs to rest."

"Is she upset about Virginia's dying? It must be hard for her, knowing the last thing they did was quarrel." Peg kept her eyes on Guy as she adjusted the coat on her shoulders and began to button it.

He shook his head. "She doesn't know about Virginia. We haven't told her. She's been so upset over losing her precious pin, we're waiting until the investigation is over before we decide how to tell her. It's best if she hears it all at once instead of fretting over unknowns."

Once they said good-bye to Guy and were back in the car, Peg took out her cell phone and Detective Ruthers' business card. Edna listened to one side of the conversation as Peg explained about the duplicate brooch.

After she'd ended the call, Peg told Edna that the detective asked her to meet him at the station. He did want to keep them for the time being, and asked if she would give her formal statement as long as she was coming in. If Edna would drop Peg off at the Division, Ruthers would see that she got home.

Before starting the car, Edna turned to Peg for reassurance. "Is it possible that your father had the copy made and you just didn't know about it? Maybe he had a replacement made after you left for college."

Peg shook her head. "He was convinced that Mother had only misplaced it. He was certain it would turn up, that she'd find she'd left it on a dress or dropped it in the closet among her shoes. He never believed that Cherisse stole it. I remember that clearly." She gave Edna a wry smile. "He kept the original drawing, but I'm positive I would have known if he'd commissioned a jeweler to make another brooch for Mother."

Edna started at the significance of what she'd just heard. "Wait a minute. Are you saying the design is still around, still available?"

Peg frowned as if the answer were obvious. "Of course. Father never threw anything away. The sketch was in the desk with his other papers. When Joey used the office, he left Father's papers alone, but Stephen wanted to use the desk for himself. He boxed up all of Father's things and probably stored them in the attic." She turned away from Edna and, settling herself more comfortably, pulled the seatbelt across her chest and buckled it, ending the conversation.

After a brief silence as she assimilated this latest discovery, Edna buckled her own seatbelt and started the car.

Chapter Eighteen

The drive between her home and Peg's had become rhythmic for Edna. Leaving Peg's neighborhood for the third time that week, she slipped into the traffic's pattern and allowed her thoughts to run over the events of the last four days. The rain had stopped earlier that afternoon and billowy white clouds drifted lazily across a pale blue sky. The cool air smelled of spring and wet pavement. Although the late afternoon was pleasant, Edna's mind was troubled.

Thoughts of rosary beads and snake venom whirled in her head and, with them, the question of who would benefit from Virginia's death and in what way? Was the murderer's motive financial or emotional? Would Stephen have given the rosary to the police if Edna hadn't forced his hand? If not, why not? Who would know enough about rosary peas to realize they could be lethal? Did the killer know about Virginia's heart condition? Why did she hide the brooch beneath her jacket lapel? *A very good hiding place.* Edna's conscious mind took a slight detour to admire the housekeeper's ingenuity before concentrating again on more immediate concerns. Who had commissioned a duplicate of the ruby, sapphire and diamond circle pin and when?

She made a mental note to look in Mrs. Rabichek's journals for more information on the rosary peas, or maybe she referred to them as precatory beans, another of their common names. Thinking of plants and gardens, her thoughts flashed to Goran and Jaycee. Had the two of them hit it off so well that they ran away together? They'd known each other for such a short time. Jaycee didn't seem like the type who would willingly hitch herself to a stranger. Why was she hiding her real identity? Why change her name? Edna wished anew that Jaycee's note hadn't been obliterated by the rain. It might have revealed where she had gone or why, and when she'd return. Obviously, she'd be back. She wouldn't simply walk away from a house and all her belongings, would she?

As Edna drew nearer to home, she made a quick decision and, passing her own driveway, turned up the slope beside Jaycee's house and parked in front of the garage. Stepping out, she went around to the side door and peered through the dusty glass panes of its top half. Light from the setting sun filtered through the row of small windows set high in the main garage door, illuminating a black-and-chrome motorcycle parked beside a red scooter, but no car. She stared at the bike, wondering what was different about it until she realized that the black leather saddlebags were missing. If Goran and Jaycee made plans to go off somewhere together, he'd use the bags as a suitcase, she decided and shrugged. She'd seen what she'd come for and that was to learn if Jaycee had returned home.

As long as she was there, Edna thought she might as well check the doors and make certain the house looked undisturbed. She climbed the stairs and crossed the deck to the back door. She looked into the kitchen through the gauze curtain covering the single, large window. Seeing nothing amiss, she tried the knob and eased her mind that the door was locked. Next, she walked around to the front door and made sure that door was also secure. She tried looking through the windows to check the front rooms, but drapes completely obliterated any view into either room. Having made the attempt, Edna was somewhat satisfied that all seemed safe and peaceful. She returned to her car and backed down the driveway to park before her own house.

Darkness had fallen by the time she slid her key into the lock and let herself in through the front door. Benjamin came scampering around the corner from the side garden and slipped inside before the door shut. She stopped only long enough to hang her coat in the closet and set her purse on the hall table before heading into the kitchen.

A note Starling had left on the table informed Edna that her daughter was with Charlie and wouldn't be home for dinner. Edna was disappointed. She'd hoped to discuss her thoughts with Starling, if only to put some perspective on the recent events. Sighing with resignation to an evening of explaining everything only to her cat, she fed him his supper. With that done, she poured herself a glass of wine and took it upstairs where she drew a hot bath.

An hour later, dressed in her long, blue

velveteen robe, she poured a second glass of wine and, with a plate of sharp cheddar cheese and homemade crackers, she went into the living room. Lighting a small fire in the grate, she sat in her favorite wing-back chair beside the hearth and stared at the flames while sipping chardonnay and nibbling crackers.

The idea of Jaycee running off with Goran didn't make any sense to her. Even if Peg's gardener were a fast mover as Starling had teased, it didn't explain Jaycee's behavior. Edna felt her young neighbor would be more cautious than to traipse off with someone she'd only just met. Had she been forced to leave? She had to be with Goran or why would his motorcycle be in her garage and her own car missing?

Edna thought of the envelope Jaycee had left in her care. On impulse, she went to her office, opened the drawer and took out the envelope. She read again what Jaycee had written on the front. "Property of J.W. If not collected within a week, please phone ..." And there was the area code for Chicago. It was the only connection she now had with her young neighbor. She wondered about dialing the number and asking whoever answered if he or she had heard from Jaycee in the last day or so.

She was staring at the envelope without really seeing it, trying to decide whether or not to phone, when a loud pounding on the front door made her jump and almost drop the packet.

"Who in the world ..." she muttered, clutching the envelope to her chest and leaving the office. The banging sounded again when she was halfway to the door, increasing her agitation and causing her to hurry the rest of the way. "Hold your horses," she shouted at the door. She was rattled by having her peace unexpectedly disturbed and impatient to see who would be knocking so viciously instead of ringing the bell. She switched on the porch light and wrenched open the door without first looking through the peek hole.

She did not recognize the man standing on her stoop, hunched against the cool of the night. The collar was turned up on his black leather jacket, partially hiding his jaw and chin. The black baseball cap pulled low over his forehead held no design and served to cover his head and shield the upper part of his face. The partial glare she was able to discern in his dark eyes was hard and gave Edna a sudden chill.

"Yes?" She flicked her eyes to the hook that was the only deterrent to the man pulling open the screen door and forcing his way into the house. "What do you want?" Some of her anger was returning, and she was glad her voice didn't quiver as the muscles of her legs seemed to be doing at the moment.

His voice was low and rough, as if he were a heavy smoker. "I'm looking for your neighbor." He pointed with his thumb, half turning to indicate Jaycee's place across the street.

"Sorry," she said, beginning to shut the door. "I can't help you."

"Saw you up at the house earlier's why I'm askin'. You know when she'll be home?" He pulled on the handle of the screen door, but the hook held. The door's clatter as he jerked on it chafed at Edna's nerves.

It was then she noticed he was staring at the envelope she held across her chest. "I don't know where she is or when she'll be back. I can't help you," she repeated.

She was stepping back and about to close the door when her attention was drawn to his hand as he unzipped his jacket and reached across his stomach to grab something attached to his belt. The sight of a knife handle mesmerized her.

"Hi, Edna. Wha'cha doin'?"

The spell broke in a rush of relief at the sound of Mary's voice. Edna looked beyond the man on her doorstep to see Mary standing in the driveway with Hank at her side. The dog was alert, tail down, but he neither barked nor growled. Clad in jungle fatigues, Mary was barely visible at the edge of the light from the porch. Her left hand rested on the dog's head. Her right was down by her side and slightly behind her thigh.

Edna's mind flashed back to the first and only time she'd seen Mary stand like that and knew instantly her neighbor was holding a gun. She didn't know whether to be frightened or relieved.

"Wha'cha doin'?" Mary's repeated words were for Edna, but her eyes never left the stranger.

The three of them stood frozen in a tableau for several heartbeats until the man backed slowly off the porch. He kept his eyes on Mary and Hank until he melted into the darkness. Edna waited until his footsteps faded down the broken-shells to the road.

"Come in, Mary. Quickly." She unlatched the hook and swung the screen door wide. When they were inside, Edna bolted the front door, before collapsing back against the heavy wood. "I've never been so happy to see anyone in my life," she said and straightened. Her heart was beating like a jack hammer. As she opened her arms to give Mary a hug, Jaycee's envelope fell to the floor.

"What's this?" Mary dodged the hug to pick up the envelope while Hank bent to sniff what he thought Edna had tossed to him. Uninterested, the dog turned to smell Benjamin instead, the cat having padded up beside him.

"It's something Jaycee asked me to keep for her," Edna said, taking the packet and heading back to the living room. "Come sit. I'll tell you about it as soon as I get you something to drink." She glanced at the gun in Mary's hand. "Please put it away. I know you know how to handle it, but it does make me nervous."

Mary took off her coat, folded it over the gun and set them on a chair just inside the arch to the living room. Edna put Jaycee's envelope on the coffee table before leaving for the kitchen. When she returned moments later, wine in hand, she saw Mary, seated on the sofa, drop the envelope back onto the coffee table.

"Have you tried the phone number," she asked, accepting the goblet Edna held out.

"Didn't have time," Edna replied, tossing

another log on the fire before resuming her chair. "I was in the office, trying to decide whether or not I *should* call, when that man started banging on the door. He scared me."

Mary took a sip of her drink, nodded and said, "Scared me, too. Hank didn't like him either." The dog was lying near Mary's feet, head on his outstretched paws, eyes alert for any morsel of cheese or crumb of cracker that might possibly hit the floor. Benjamin was curled up in a bed beside the hearth.

It was a peaceful scene and Edna's nerves were beginning to calm when Hank's head jerked up and a low growl began deep in his throat. He was struggling to his feet when a deep voice said, "Hold him or he's dead."

As Mary grabbed Hank's collar, Edna saw Benjamin streak off to hide in a far corner of the room. At the same time, she whipped her head around and saw the darkly-clad stranger standing in the archway, holding a gun. His collar was still up around his chin and mouth and his cap pulled low on his forehead. All she could see of his face were cold, dark eyes, a nose that had been broken more than once, and lips twisted in a snarl. Inches from his right knee was the chair on which Mary had left her pistol.

"Toss me that envelope," he growled, wobbling his weapon in the direction of the coffee table. "Do it and I won't have to shoot you."

Edna started to stand, but he stopped her. "Sit down. Pick it up and throw it over here. Careful like."

She did as she was told, tossing the packet as her granddaughter had taught her to throw a Frisbee, only with less force behind her wrist. She wished she dared throw it at his face. The envelope landed about a foot from his shoes which she noticed were scuffed and rubber soled. With her artist's eye, she was trying to remember every detail she could in order to sketch him later for Charlie and the police. She knew she'd get the eyes right. It would take many days and not a few nightmares to forget the evil in them.

The gunman bent and picked up the envelope without taking his eyes from the group near the fireplace. He turned it over and quickly glanced at the back flap with its metal clasp and clear, package tape still in place. Waving the envelope in the air and keeping his eyes on the two women, he began to back out of the room. "Good thing you girls didn't peek," he said. "That means I don't have to kill ya."

The corners of his eyes crinkled in what Edna guessed must be a smile, but looked more like a sneer. "Should lock your doors at night," he said in a mocking tone. "Never know who might walk in." His voice hardened when he added, "Stay put and count to a hun'red. If you move before that, you're dead. Get the picture?" With a short bark of a laugh as if enjoying a joke, he back away without waiting for a reply.

Edna half expected Mary to jump up and run after him and was amazed to see her calmly lift her glass off the coffee table and take a sip of wine. She was surprised but also relieved that her courageous neighbor wasn't dashing up to grab her gun. Too stunned and frightened to speak at first, Edna finally squeaked, "Do you think he's gone? We need to call Charlie."

Mary caught Edna's look and shook her head. She still held Hank firmly by the collar. "Yes, he's probably gone, but wait here until I check the doors." She pushed herself up from the sofa, heeled the dog and, on her way out of the living room, picked up her gun. She was back in a few minutes, Hank still at her side.

"Back door was wide open. He must have come in that way, but it wasn't jimmied. No sign he broke in."

Edna winced. "Starling must have left it unlocked for me. We've gotten into that habit when we know someone will be home soon. I didn't think to check it when I came in the front door this evening."

Mary rolled her eyes, but said only, "Both doors're shut and locked now."

Edna was too weak with relief that they hadn't been hurt to be offended by Mary's unspoken criticism of the Davieses' lax security measures. "I hope there was nothing too important in that envelope of Jaycee's."

"Whatever is in it is probably on this too," Mary said, reaching inside the breast pocket of her shirt and removing a small black wafer. She held it up between thumb and forefinger, grinning broadly.

Chapter Nineteen

"Where did you get that," Edna demanded, a feeling of dread beginning to burn the pit of her stomach. Mary was too pleased with herself, by far.

"The tape only covered part of the flap. I felt a bulge near the clasp so I stuck my pen knife in to see what it was." Mary's eyes went wide with innocence. "This just fell out."

She put the wafer in the palm of her hand and extended it toward Edna who stared at it transfixed before stuttering, "Starling uses those. It's one of those what-cha-ma-call-its ... a memory chip for a digital camera."

"That's right. It's like the one I use in my digital," Mary said. "That's why I think whatever's in the envelope might also be on this chip. That guy thought he got away with it, but I fooled him." Mary's grin grew wider.

Edna felt her skin growing cold and clammy. Her stomach wasn't feeling so hot either. "And what happens when he doesn't find it in the envelope?"

"He probably doesn't know what was in it in the first place." Mary shrugged. "He's just a messenger. Even if he did know what to expect, he won't open it. His boss would probably have to kill him if he did."

"And what if this *boss* is waiting down the road? That thug could be back any minute."

"Bosses don't wait near the scene of a crime," Mary said with confidence.

"I've got to call Charlie." Realizing the futility of arguing with her all-things-criminal-enthusiast neighbor, Edna headed for her office, turning back when she heard a commotion behind her. Mary was close on her heels with Hank beside her. Benjamin, seeing everyone leaving the room, crawled cautiously from his hiding place in the corner and trotted after them. *Safety in numbers*, Edna thought, turning back and hiding a smile. She would have felt cheered if she weren't so worried about an angry gunman outside her house.

As soon as she entered her office and flicked on the overhead light, Edna crossed to the window and lowered the shade, something she almost never did. Even though prowlers had broken in the previous fall, they'd been caught. Knowing who the felons were and that the break-ins weren't liable to happen again, she'd felt safe in the neighborhood. A screening of laurel and lilac bushes hid her house from cars going by along the road, so she hadn't thought it necessary to pull every shade in the house after dark.

Feeling a little more secure after shutting out the night, she moved to the desk, picked up the phone and dialed Charlie's cell number. He answered on the fifth ring.

"Rogers."

She was surprised she sounded as calm as she did with her stomach tied in a million knots. Still, her voice shook slightly when she said, "Charlie, it's Edna. Mary and I were just threatened at gun point. Our intruder may not have left the neighborhood yet. Would you come and check?"

Police Detective Charlie Rogers knew her well enough from past experience not to waste time questioning her. "Stay put. I'll call for a patrol and be there as soon as I can, no more than fifteen minutes." The words were barely out of his mouth before he hung up.

True to his word, he arrived twelve minutes later with Starling in tow. Edna and Mary had stayed in the office with the dog and cat. Once Charlie assured himself they were unharmed, he put his hand in the small of Starling's back and gently propelled her into the room. "I'm going out to talk to the patrol and look around. I think it would be best if you ladies stay in this room until I get back." At a nod of reassurance and approval from Edna, he hurried from the room, flipping open his cell phone as he disappeared into the hall.

"What happened? Are you okay?" Starling rushed to hug her mother, then straightened to look questioningly at Mary. Hank pushed his nose into Starling's hand, and she scratched his ears absently as she waited to hear the details of their evening.

"So what happened," she asked when nobody spoke up. She rested a hip on the desk as Edna sat back in her swivel chair. Mary, sitting in the straight-back chair beside the desk, held up the memory chip for Starling to see.

"Got something to read this with?"

Starling frowned in puzzlement, but

answered, "Sure. What is it?"

"Memory chip from a camera," Mary said.

Starling rolled her eyes skyward. "I know *that*," she said lowering her eyes to meet Mary's twinkling ones. "I meant what's on it?"

"Don't know. We need to look."

When Starling turned a questioning gaze on her mother, Edna explained about the envelope that Jaycee had left in her care. "That man must have seen what was written on the front when I opened the door to him earlier this evening. That's why he came back." She shook her head in disgust. "I should have left it in the desk."

"Don't kick yourself, Mom. How were you to know?" Starling pushed away from the desk. "I'll run upstairs and get my laptop."

Edna was about to protest that Charlie wanted them to stay in the office, but she too was curious to see what the chip held. Until her daughter reappeared in the doorway, computer in hand, she didn't realize she'd hardly taken a breath, hoping the man with the gun hadn't somehow reentered the house and hidden upstairs. She wouldn't feel easy until she knew he'd been caught.

She gave her seat to her daughter and Starling set her laptop on the desk, pushing Edna's monitor aside to make room. While the computer booted up, she slid a camera bag from her shoulder and rummaged for an adapter which she plugged into one of the USB ports. Mary handed over the chip, having moved her chair around to sit as close as she could get to watch the screen.

Edna stood behind her daughter, as mesmerized as Mary, waiting for a display of the contents of the little black wafer.

Starling slipped the memory chip into the adapter and began to swipe a finger across the touch pad to position the cursor and then press buttons to start programs and open windows. Suddenly, a photo appeared showing a large three-story house with flames shooting around the lower windows and above the front door. Black soot crawled up the white clapboard walls as the fire reached for upper floors. The three women watched in horror as a grisly slideshow scrolled across the screen showing how the fire had engulfed the house.

"These must be the pictures Carol James took of the fire in Chicago, the ones the magazine article described," Starling said, her eyes not moving from the screen.

At the end of the fire series were several images that had obviously been cropped from sections of other pictures. Starling ran her fingers over the keyboard and touch pad to change the display to thumbnail images of the contents of the camera chip. Pointing and clicking on one, she enlarged the photo of a man looking over his shoulder.

"That's one of the pictures that sent the arsonist to prison. It was in the magazine article after the trial."

The man had a scowl on his face, as if he'd heard something and was looking back to see who was behind him. Carol James, a.k.a. Jaycee

Watkins, had shot the photos with a long lens from a copse of trees across the residential street from the house, Starling explained to the others.

"Bring up those small pictures again," Edna said, leaning over Starling's shoulder. "I think I saw something."

When the images appeared, she put her finger on one. "Can you make this one larger?"

As Starling obliged, a shadow could be seen. The image was a blowup of the corner of one of the early shots when the flames hadn't thrown as much light over the front yard. Light from a street lamp must have created the blurred silhouette. The arsonist who had been tried and convicted had been in a different spot in the same photo, so the shadow was not his. Starling brought up another enlargement that displayed a grainy image of the same section of wall. Barely discernable, it was either an optical illusion or a second man had been on the scene.

"Do you suppose it could be our visitor," Mary asked, twisting her head to look up at Edna.

"Maybe. It would explain why he was looking for Jaycee and why he was so interested in the envelope."

Starling said with excitement in her voice, "It looks like these pictures prove there were two arsonists at the fire, but only one man was brought to trial." She tapped keys and swiped at the touch pad. "I want to take these back to my studio and see if I can find anything else. I know Carol ..." she hesitated, "... or Jaycee or whatever her name is--probably went over these with a fine tooth comb, but maybe fresh eyes will see something else."

"You can't take that. Charlie will want the chip," Edna reminded her.

"He can have the chip. I'm just copying the contents to my hard drive," Starling said, busy at her task.

"Who can have what chip?" Charlie had entered the room in time to hear Starling's last remarks. Without waiting for an answer, he spoke to the question on three faces turned his way. "Didn't find him. He's gone. There's nobody around who shouldn't be and no strange vehicles, according to the patrol."

"Edna thinks he'll be back," Mary said, sounding as if she knew better and Edna's concern was silly.

"Of course he will," Edna snapped, worry making her testy. "Whoever sees the pictures in the envelope--and I'm assuming that's what it contained--must certainly want the originals or negatives or whatever you call what's on a camera chip."

"Would someone fill me in? What envelope? What chip? Why did a man with a gun break in and threaten you two?" Charlie looked from Mary to Edna, a stern, no-nonsense expression on his face.

Edna repeated the same story she'd told Starling, about Jaycee leaving the envelope with her and how the man at the door must have seen it. When she'd finished, Charlie thought for a minute while he absently watched Mary scratch Hank's ears. Benjamin had crawled into Starling's lap and was allowing her to stroke his back.

They all watched him and waited until he broke the silence. "Edna's probably right about this guy coming back, and even if she isn't, 'better safe than sorry' as the saying goes."

"I want to get back to Boston to the studio and see if I can get anything else out of these pictures," Starling spoke up, taking the chip from the adapter and holding it up to Charlie. "I've copied everything on it to my laptop."

Instead of taking it from her, he took a small notebook from his inside coat pocket and ripped out a blank page. Starling laid the wafer on the paper and Charlie wrapped it carefully before putting it and the notebook back in his pocket.

"There's probably nothing on this, but just in case," he said. "I don't want the lab boys on my back because they found one of *my* fingerprints on it." He turned to Edna. "Can you go to Boston with Starling and stay for a few days?"

"I could follow her up in my car, but let me first check with Peg. If she can use my help, I'll stay with her."

Charlie put a hand on her arm before she could leave the room. "I'd like to keep your car here in the driveway, if you don't mind."

It took only a few seconds for Edna to reason out why. "You think he'll be back, too." It was a rhetorical question.

"It's a possibility. If your car is here, he might try to get into the house to get to you. If he tries to break in again, he'll be cautious to avoid alerting you and that might delay him long enough for the patrol to spot him."

"I can watch for him, too" Mary chimed in. "I've got new night-vision goggles."

Starling giggled and punched Mary lightly on the arm. "You're so prepared," she said with a smile as Mary grinned back at her.

"I know it's useless to ask you to stay away." Charlie looked sternly at Mary, but Edna noticed a twitch at the corner of his mouth as he hid a smile.

She thought for a moment. "I guess I can leave my car here. If Peg needs me, Starling can drop me off on her way home. Peg won't mind driving me back once you tell me it's safe."

"Benjy can come home with Hank and me," Mary volunteered.

"Benjamin," Edna corrected automatically, still looking at Charlie.

"Can I borrow a house key," he asked, ignoring the interchange. "I'll make a periodic check inside."

She nodded, feeling a cold shiver run down her spine at the thought of the stranger waiting somewhere in the house for her to return. Moving to the kitchen to get a spare key, she called Peg who, as it turned out, was not only delighted to have the company but desperate for some assistance.

"Virginia's sister is driving down from New Hampshire on Sunday. I know Virginia's friends will want to meet Janette and her husband, so I'm arranging a small memorial service at the house. I contacted Virginia's priest. He said he'll ask the church women to spread the word, and he's certain they'll bring enough food for a small army, so I won't have to worry about that. But I need to clean the house and order flowers and decide what sort of drinks to provide--and since tomorrow's Friday, I've got only two days to get things done." Beginning to sound beleaguered, Peg added, "Oh and there's more packing to do. You may be sorry you asked, but yes, I would love for you to visit for a few days."

When Edna returned to the office with Peg's answer, Starling went to get the rest of her equipment and her clothes. Mary called to Hank and Benjamin, going out through the mudroom so she could grab some cat food from the pantry on the way. Edna stopped for a minute to speak with Charlie before going upstairs to pack a small bag for what she hoped wouldn't be more than a two- or three-day stay in Providence.

"What else have you found out?"

He was leaning against the desk, examining the cell phone in his hands and studiously avoiding her eyes.

When he didn't answer immediately, she persisted. "Have you heard from your friend Dietz? What's the story with Jaycee? It's become obvious that dangerous people are looking for her. Is that why Dietz wanted you to keep an eye on her, to see that she's safe?"

His gaze flicked to her face and quickly dropped again. "I haven't talked to Dietz. He's still not answering his phone." Charlie pushed away from the desk, slipping the phone into his pocket and, taking hold of Edna's shoulders, looked her in the eyes. "I'm sorry we put you in danger. I had no idea someone would come to your house, let alone threaten you at gunpoint."

She looked at the concern in his hazel eyes for a long moment before she said, "I don't blame you. I know you couldn't have anticipated what happened tonight." Changing the subject slightly, she said, "Have you found out anything more about Goran Pittlani? Could he be in cahoots with our gunman?"

Without hesitation, Charlie shook his head, then dropped his hands and turned sideways to stare out to the hallway, effectively avoiding her eyes once more. "Your visitor wouldn't have come here looking for Jaycee if he knew Pittlani had taken her off somewhere."

"So you know for certain they're together, Jaycee and Goran?"

He looked back at her. "It seems pretty obvious. Her car is gone and his bike is in her garage. I thought we'd already agreed that they've gone off together."

Something in his reply made Edna suspect Charlie knew more than he was letting on, but before she could question him further, Starling appeared in the door with a camera bag in one hand and a small suitcase in the other. "I'm ready whenever you are, Mom."

Chapter Twenty

In less than half an hour, Edna and Starling were on their way to Providence. By the time they reached Peg's house it was nearly eleven o'clock. Starling double-parked on the street while Edna rolled her suitcase up to the front door where Peg was waiting. Starling then waved goodbye to her mother and her honorary aunt and drove off.

"I hope my staying with you for a few days won't disturb Stephen," Edna said, pulling her wheeled bag across the foyer's wood floor toward the wide staircase.

"He's out," Peg said. She turned away abruptly, but not before Edna saw tears in her best friend's eyes.

Edna chose not to question Peg in the foyer, but instead followed her up the stairs. They turned left at the landing and entered the bedroom where Peg sat in a cushioned rocker near the window while Edna unpacked and put her toiletries in the bathroom. When she'd finished, Edna sat on the edge of the bed to face Peg. Earlier, when they'd spoken on the phone, she'd explained only that there had been a break-in and would Peg mind putting her up for a night or two. Now, briefly and with as little emotion as possible so as not to alarm her friend too much, she told of the night's adventure.

"Oh, my heavens," Peg exclaimed, rapidly patting her chest with one hand when Edna reached the part where the man had crept into the house and surprised them. She decided not to mention the gun unless Peg asked why they hadn't defended themselves. "How creepy," she murmured with a shudder when Edna explained that Charlie would search the house periodically in case the stranger managed to slip inside again.

As Edna finished her narrative, describing what they'd found on the memory chip, Peg frowned. "Who is this neighbor of yours and how does she know my gardener?"

"That's the sixty-four-thousand-dollar question," Edna said. "Didn't you tell me that Stephen hired Goran for you?" At Peg's nod, she asked. "How exactly did that come about?"

"It was after I'd found the box of old photographs. I was showing them to Virginia one afternoon. We had them spread out on the dining room table when Stephen came home from work. I said I thought it would be nice to have some of the old gardens back. The yard looked so plain and Mother's gardens were so pretty, even in the black and white photos. Next thing I knew, probably a week later, Goran knocked on the door and said my husband had sent him."

"How did Stephen find him? Did he advertise?"

Peg shrugged. "I have no idea. Stephen never said and I haven't thought to ask Goran."

"Speaking of Stephen," Edna began and purposely stopped for Peg to pick up the conversation.

Peg lowered her head and fell silent for a

long moment. When Edna noticed tears wetting Peg's cheeks, she pushed herself off the bed and knelt beside the chair, looking up into Peg's face. "What is it? What's wrong?"

Peg tried to smile. Reaching into a pocket, she sputtered, "Darn. I need a tissue." She rose abruptly and headed for the bathroom, returning almost immediately with the entire box. Without preamble, she said, "I've asked Stephen to leave."

Edna's first reaction was relief, followed immediately by guilt, then sadness for her friend's obvious misery. She got up off her knees and sat back down on the bed as Peg returned to the chair. "Why? Is this sudden?"

Peg shook her head. "It's been building up, but seems to have gotten worse in the last few months. He's always at work and, when he's not, he's become controlling and dictatorial." She blew her nose as unhappiness turned to anger. "He's not the man I married, the man who wined and dined me and took me on long walks and talked for hours about a book we'd both read. I know I vowed 'for better or for worse' but lately there is no 'better'."

"Are you absolutely certain your marriage is over?"

"No, I'm not, but I want him to realize I'm serious. I will not live under his absolute rule and will no longer put up with his moods."

The two women stared at each other for another minute, as if they might conjure up answers in the air between them. Finally, Peg shook herself, breaking the spell. "I don't want to talk about it anymore tonight." She seemed to make an effort to appear more cheerful. "Are you dog tired? Would you like me to leave so you can go to bed?"

Edna gave a wry smile. "I'll probably crash in another hour or two after all the adrenalin that's been pumping through my body, but at the moment, I'm still a little on edge." Jokingly, she said, "Shall we jog around the block?"

Peg chuckled. "I have a better idea for physical exercise. I've organized things in Virginia's rooms so her sister only has to go through and let me know what she wants to keep. I've left out boxes and newspapers, so it won't take long to crate the rest. What she doesn't want, we can cart off to the local women's shelter and Goodwill. The only big thing left to do is to go through the attic to see if Virginia stored anything up there."

Inwardly, Edna groaned, thinking of the jumble of discards and dust in her own attic when they'd moved out of their old house a year ago. She kept her expression neutral, though, and pushed herself off the bed. "Let's go look."

The top floor was accessed through a door in Peg's office, across the hall from the guest bedroom. As they entered the room, Peg stopped to rummage in a desk drawer. Pulling out a large flashlight, she said, "We'll need this. There are a couple of ceiling lights up there, but they aren't very bright." She preceded Edna up narrow steps into the gloom.

When Peg flicked a wall switch, light from

a hanging bulb cast a dim glow that didn't quite reach into the attic's corners. Two large brick structures rose from the floor and extended through the roof, sectioning the room into three parts. Edna estimated the chimneys and each end of the attic lay above the respective bedrooms on the second floor. The area between the chimney pieces would be over the foyer and staircase. A soft radiance along the slanted roofline indicated two more low-wattage bulbs hanging from the ceiling in each section.

Peg had moved to a floor lamp standing out from the wall halfway between the stairwell and a window at the end of the room. She turned it on, casting a more effective brilliance on the boxes and shelves in that part of the attic.

Edna stared around her in amazement. "I have never seen such a well organized storage space in my life."

Peg grinned with pleasure. "Well, perhaps 'cluttered but clean' would be the best description. Mother's training. She insisted that nothing be put up here that wasn't carefully labeled. She also insisted we arrange things in logical groups. I'm afraid I haven't kept up with her plan religiously, but there's still some method to the madness. Mostly, you'll find old furniture and boxes from my parents' day back there at the opposite end. Geoff's childhood toys and books are all in the middle, along with his father's belongings. I haven't thrown a lot of things away, hoping Geoff will sort through them eventually."

Edna said, "It's not as dusty as I expected,

but like all old attics, it's stuffy. Can we open a window?"

"Good idea. I'll get the one at this end. You take the flashlight. Start at the far end and work your way back to me. I don't think Virginia would have stored anything except in this area but let's make sure. She came up here periodically, mostly to clean, but she may have rearranged some things. I'll look through the boxes and shelves here."

Obligingly, Edna set off with renewed energy after seeing how orderly and relatively dust-free the attic was. As Peg predicted, the rear space contained assorted pieces of furniture-- chairs with broken legs or ripped upholstery, tables with a cracked leaf or deep scratch, lamps with torn shades or frayed cords. She moved quickly, seeing nothing marked with Virginia's name and assuming the furniture had belonged to Peg's family and not the housekeeper.

In the center section, she smiled at some of the discarded toys and sports equipment from Geoff's youth. A boy's tricycle with one back wheel missing leaned against the outer wall. A baseball bat lay across two boxes. The glove must be around somewhere, she thought, remembering the Little League games she and Peg had sat through with their sons. She smiled, happy with the thought that the two boys, men now, had remained best friends. On a whim, she lifted the bat and looked into one of the boxes beneath. Sure enough, an old, scarred baseball glove rested on top of a stack of games and books. She pulled it out and reclosed the lid.

Her younger son Grant was bringing his family from Colorado to visit in another couple of months. Remembering how much fun her nine-year-old granddaughter Jillian had teaching her how to throw a Frisbee, Edna thought the child might enjoy learning some basics about baseball. She'd ask Peg to borrow the bat and glove, but she'd buy a new ball.

With her mind on Grant's visit, Edna started around the chimney to join Peg at the top of the steps in the most cluttered section of the attic. She was about to call out, "Look what I found," when she heard a deep voice from the stairs.

"Whaa're you doin' up here?"

Following an instinct, Edna moved quietly back into the shadows.

Stephen's head, then his shoulders, rose slowly and unsteadily out of the stairwell until he was standing in the room. Edna had never seen him look so disheveled. The left sleeve of his white dress shirt was turned back at the cuff while the right sleeve was rolled all the way to his elbow. His shirt tail was pulling loose from his black suit pants, and his hair was mussed on one side, as if he'd raked it with his fingers. Leaning slightly forward and squinting at his wife, he repeated in a slightly slurred, but demanding voice, "Whaa're you doin'?"

"You're drunk, Stephen." Peg sounded annoyed and not at all sympathetic. "Go to bed. I came up here to see if there's anything belonging to Virginia."

He twisted from the waist, leaving his feet planted and reaching out to steady himself on the top of a stack of boxes. As he looked erratically around the room, Edna stood perfectly still. Holding her breath, she hoped, between the shadows in the attic and the amount he'd had to drink, that he wouldn't spot her. His behavior was making her feel uneasy, and she wished she'd stuck her cell phone in her pocket before coming upstairs.

Eventually, his gaze fixed on Peg, and he frowned as if trying to remember why they were both standing in the attic.

"Stephen!" Peg's voice was harsh as she stepped closer to him and grabbed his arm. "Please go down stairs before you fall and hurt yourself."

He swung his arms up and away in a swimmer's breast-stroke motion, breaking her hold on his bicep. As his arms circled back around, his palms were facing outward in front of his chest. He pushed out, fiercely striking her shoulders. "Don't touch me," he growled. "You've ruined everything."

"What are you talking about?" Peg had stumbled backward at his attack, but caught herself before she fell. "What is the matter with you," she said, a note of fear starting to creep into her voice.

Stephen descended on her and struck her again with his palms to her shoulders. As she staggered another few steps backwards, he shouted, "You have no idea how hard it is to run a bank, the problems I have to deal with. You and your high-and-mighty friends, sitting around with your tea and your gossip while I have to deal with the *real* world. And now you want me to leave. I'm not good enough for you, is that it?"

Peg sounded stern when she said, "You don't know what you're saying. We'll discuss this when you've sobered up."

Her words seemed to fuel his anger. "I know exactly what I'm saying," he snarled as he lurched toward her. "I won't let you destroy my bank." Again he struck, forcing her back with each slap to her shoulders.

"Stop it, Stephen. You're hurting me." Peg's voice was now filled with both confusion and fear.

"I won't go away quietly and lose everything I've worked for." His anger was building. "You have no idea of the pressure I'm under."

"I might if you'd talk to me, but I won't listen when you're this drunk." Peg stepped back another foot as Stephen advanced on her.

Unlike her friend whose mind was distracted by the husband's onslaught, Edna saw what was happening. Close to panic, she yelled, "Look out, Peg. Behind you."

Peg half turned to see she was only about two feet from the window. The lower half, reaching from mid-calf to hip, was open to the night. The frame looked old and brittle. She spun back, wild-eyed, as Stephen pushed her again. As she fell backwards and her shoulder slammed into the panes of the upper half, a resounding crack of wood and glass echoed in the room.

Stephen hadn't turned when Edna called out. The thought flicked through her mind that he was so enraged at Peg, he didn't register another presence. More concerned with her friend, she wondered with growing horror how long the structure would hold up if he kept knocking Peg against it.

Seconds earlier, when Stephen began to shout at Peg, Edna had dropped the baseball glove, but had hung onto the bat. Now, leaving the shadow of the chimney, she moved quickly up behind him, raising the bat to her shoulder. When she was almost upon him, with one fluid motion, she pivoted and swung as if going for a ground ball. It was at least a two-base hit as she connected with the side of his knee.

The crack of wood hitting bone was followed by a high-pitched scream as he fell sideways into a pile of boxes. Cartons flew in all directions under his weight. He lay on his back, clutching his leg and howling. Confusion turned to surprise when he finally seemed aware of Edna. He gaped up at her a second before his face contorted in agony.

Even though he was yelling loud enough to shake the rafters, she was disappointed by the realization that the alcohol he'd consumed must be dulling some of the pain. *He deserves to feel every stab and twitch after what he'd nearly done to Peg*, she thought.

Trying to catch her breath and with one hand against the wall for support, Peg stared from her husband to her friend and back again. Her face pinched in disbelief. "He almost pushed me out the window." She began to tremble. "He might have killed me."

Not wanting to lose her to shock, Edna said sternly, "Go downstairs and call for an ambulance."

Peg stared blankly as if not understanding the words.

Edna knew she had to keep her friend from falling apart, if only for a little while. "Listen to me, Peg. You must go dial nine-one-one. Stephen needs a doctor, and he'll need help getting down the stairs. Neither of us is going to get close to him. Do you understand?"

Peg blinked stupidly for another few seconds before nodding slowly. "Yes. Alright." She eyed her husband carefully as she pushed herself erect and sidled past him. Only when she was well out of his reach did she turn and hurry down to the office. Edna was left to guard Stephen as he rocked back and forth, groaning and holding his leg just above the damaged knee. He scowled warily at the bat in her hand and didn't attempt to get up. If he wondered how Edna had come to be in the attic, he didn't ask.

A minute or two later, Peg's voice, sounding steady and controlled, rose from below. "Will you be okay, Ed? An ambulance is on the way. I have to let them in when they get here."

"Go," Edna shouted back, glaring at

Stephen with a fury she'd not felt before in her life. "I'll be fine."

Chapter Twenty-One

The next hour passed in a haze for Edna. Once the ambulance arrived and the EMTs were attending to Stephen, she could allow herself to relax. As she did so, she began to tremble with relief and fatigue. Testing several nearby boxes, she found one sturdy enough to hold her weight and sank gratefully on top. Peg stood nearby, watching two white-clad men load her husband onto a stretcher.

When the technicians had Stephen firmly strapped to the gurney, they moved slowly down the stairs with Peg following. Everyone ignored Stephen's howls of pain, one or two of which Edna suspected were more for effect than wrenched from agony. Dreading the thought of remaining alone in the attic, she mustered the strength to get down the steps. By the time she reached the office, she felt somewhat stronger. As her main thought switched to Peg, Edna resolutely shut the door to the attic and went down to the foyer where, having seen the emergency team out, Peg had collapsed against the front door. Her eyes were closed and she seemed to be as dazed as Edna felt.

As Edna drew near, Peg opened her eyes. "Do you suppose he's badly hurt? I can't imagine you hit him that hard."

"Hard enough." Flailing her hands at her sides, Edna shuddered. "Ugh. I'll probably feel the vibration of bat hitting bone for a long time."

"I'm exhausted, but I don't think I'll be able to sleep tonight."

"Do you have any brandy?"

Some of the old Peg returned when she said, "We do, if Stephen didn't drink it all." Her smile didn't reach her eyes, however, and she added, "Sorry. Bad joke."

Edna put an arm around Peg's shoulders as they both turned toward the dining room. "It's okay. It's just the two of us. Say whatever you like. I think we both need to air our thoughts, if we both agree to forget everything that's said in the next hour. Remember when we did that in college? Forget all and forgive all when we needed to clear our heads?" She patted Peg's back. "Come on. I think a lot of brandy in a little warm milk might be just the thing to make us sleepy."

This time Peg's smile did bring a twinkle to her eyes and putting an arm around Edna's waist, gave her a one-arm hug. She stopped at the side board to grab a bottle of the liquor while Edna went through to the kitchen.

When they were both seated at the kitchen table with the warm drinks in front of them, Edna felt the tension in her muscles ease a little. Several minutes passed before Peg broke the silence. "Do you think he really meant to push me out the window?"

Hesitating as she waivered between a truthful or a tactful reply, Edna finally shook her head, deciding on tact, since she wasn't at all certain what Stephen's intentions had been. She didn't want Peg to dwell on that line of thinking, however, so she asked, "What did he mean when he said 'I won't let you destroy my bank.'?"

"I have no idea." Peg sipped at her milk-laced brandy.

"You mentioned earlier that you've asked him to leave. Is he afraid he'll lose the bank in a divorce settlement?"

Peg shook her head. "Most of our assets are separate. In the two years we've been married, we haven't acquired much common property. According to our prenup, I have no claims on his bank or his income, just as he has no rights to this house or any of my money."

"You signed a prenuptial agreement?"

"Geoff thought it would be a good idea." She hesitated before adding, "He's never really been fond of Stephen. He's tried to hide his feelings from me, but I've always thought Geoff wouldn't like anyone who took his father's place."

Edna thought Peg's son would accept a more fun loving or emotionally compatible partner for Peg, as would she and Albert, but didn't want to pursue that line of conversation either. Instead, she said, "How are you feeling? Would you like some more brandy and milk?"

"Why not?" Peg grinned and nearly looked like her old self. Some color had even returned to her cheeks. "I think another might allow me to sleep, if I can crawl my way up to the bedroom."

They both laughed, and Edna rose to refill their mugs.

A half hour later, as she turned off the

bedside lamp, an earlier question of Peg's popped into her head. *Had Stephen knowingly been trying to push Peg out the window?* No answer came to her, and the last thing she remembered that night was the cool softness of the pillow beneath her cheek.

It was past ten o'clock the next morning before she awoke. The wonderfully drowsy feeling induced by milk and brandy the night before had been replaced with a slight headache. Rolling out of bed, she took a long hot shower and dressed in comfortable, green wool slacks and a white turtle-neck. Still feeling a chill that went all the way to her bones, she grabbed a sweater of multiple earth tones and pulled it over her jersey. In the kitchen, she found Peg sitting at the table, warming her hands around a coffee mug. Elbows on the table, she was staring out the window at the backyard as Edna entered the room.

"Mornin', Ed." When Peg turned to greet her, the dark circles beneath her eyes made her look worse than Edna felt. "Help yourself to coffee. That's a fresh pot."

"Were you able to sleep at all," Edna asked, pouring a cup and bringing it to the table.

Peg shook her head and bit her lip. "Not much." Tears welled in her eyes, but didn't spill over. After a minute of silence in which Edna knew her friend was trying to gain control of her emotions, Peg said, "I've been trying to understand what possessed Stephen last night. I've never known him to look or act like that. He was a complete stranger to me."

The tears did fall then, silently drifting down her cheeks as she looked at Edna to provide impossible answers.

"Why don't I make you some toast. You look exhausted. Maybe if you eat something and lie down, you'll be able to sleep for a little while. We'll talk later."

"I don't think I could, Ed."

Not knowing if Peg meant eat or sleep or both, Edna ignored her and rose to make toast from a loaf of homemade bread she found in the bread box. Rummaging in the refrigerator, she came out with a partially-used jar of homemade, strawberry jam which she spread liberally on the toast before setting the plate in front of Peg. She thought the extra sugar would be good for the shock Peg must be feeling. She made herself the same breakfast and when they both had finished, she persuaded Peg to lie down on the couch in the library. This morning, she lit the fire in the hearth before sitting in the rocker and reaching for the copy of "Little Women" she'd left on the side table.

So much had happened since she'd put the book down the afternoon before. Looking at the printed pages, her mind wasn't on the story, but on the previous evening's events. Why *had* Stephen been acting so crazy? Try as she might, Edna could not fathom a logical reason for his behavior except to wonder if he'd gone completely mad. She finally decided to force herself into the story on her lap and try to free her mind of the inexplicable happenings in the world around her.

She was startled awake by the repeated chiming of the doorbell. The book had fallen from her lap and the fire had burned down to a few smoldering embers. As she rose from the rocker feeling a little muzzy-headed, she glanced at the mantle piece clock and was surprised to see it was nearly two o'clock. Noticing Peg's eyes were open, she said, "I'll see who that is. Try to go back to sleep."

But Peg threw the afghan aside and sat up, looking and sounding groggy. "Let's both go see who it is. I need to move around, clear my head. A little sleep is almost as bad as none at all." She smiled wanly and held out a hand for Edna to help her up.

The doorbell chimed again as the two women entered the foyer. Peg opened the door to a grim-faced Detective Ruthers.

"Why ... hello, Detective," Peg said, sounding puzzled at his being there. Then, as if understanding dawned, she said, "Have you found out who copied Mother's brooch?"

"Yes, but that's not the only reason I'm here. When I got to the Division this morning, I heard about a complaint." He nodded at Edna. "Seems you attacked Mr. Bishop last night. That right?"

Edna wasn't certain if she saw one side of his mouth twitch upward when she said, "Yes, sir. I did."

Ruthers looked back at Peg. "Is there somewhere we can sit and talk?"

She led the way back to the library after

the detective declined the offer of coffee or tea. Once they were seated, Peg and Edna on the sofa with Ruthers in the rocker next to the fireplace, he said without preamble, "What happened here last night."

"Have you spoken with my husband?"

Ruthers nodded. "Went to see him at the hospital this morning."

"What did he say?"

"I'd like to hear it from you, Mrs. Bishop." He sat back and folded his hands in his lap, waiting.

After staring at him for several seconds as if expecting the detective to change his mind and tell her what Stephen had said, Peg began her recital with the reason she and Edna had gone to the attic. She completed her story with the 911 call for an ambulance. Edna sat quietly throughout and watched to see if Ruthers would give away anything by his facial expressions. He didn't. She thought she'd not like to play poker with him, amusing herself at the absurdity of the idea. *Really, I must keep my mind on the matter at hand*, she thought.

A minute or two passed after Peg finished speaking before Ruthers pulled two small plastic bags from his jacket pocket and laid them on the coffee table in front of them. Each bag held one of the circle pins that had been the object of so much recent controversy.

"One is a copy," he said, pulling the rocker closer to the table. Peg looked up with a frown. "We know. The one with the bent backing is the copy. Right?"

Feeling a twinge of impatience with the detective, Edna said, "We'd already figured that's what it must be. What we'd like to know is who had it made and when."

"Mr. Bishop commissioned the fake," Ruthers said, turning one over to show them the damaged clasp. "We located the jeweler who said he made it from a pen-and-ink design your husband showed him. We uncovered that bit of information late yesterday. I was planning to drop by today to talk to both you and your husband, Mrs. Bishop, but of course my plans changed with the events of last night."

"Stephen?" Peg spoke the name as a question, then said numbly, "Stephen had this made?"

"That's correct. Apparently your husband has had copies made of many pieces of your jewelry. Fairly good copies, but fakes, nonetheless. We had a long talk this morning in his hospital room. He's decided to cooperate and gave us permission to examine the contents of his safe deposit box."

"Why would he do that?" Peg stared at the detective as if not understanding what he was saying. "Why would he copy my jewelry?"

"He's been paying extortion money to some pretty nasty fellows. Apparently, he couldn't bring himself to embezzle bank funds, but he didn't think you'd notice if he switched your jewelry for decent replacements. Said you didn't wear them much anyway."

"That's why he insisted on keeping everything at the bank," Peg said, staring down at the pins on the table and seemingly speaking to herself.

"You say someone was extorting money. Who was threatening him?" Edna spoke up, more interested in the cause of Stephen's betrayal.

"A small but well-organized bunch of cheap hoods, operating out of Chicago. They've hit small banks in five large cities from Chicago to Boston, according to the Treasury department. These sharks get someone, preferably the bank president, to lend them large sums with questionable pay-back terms. When the note comes due, our upstanding citizens refuse to pay and it turns out their collateral is phony. Any banker who tries to collect or bring in the authorities ends up in the hospital or worse. There's at least one case of a home being burned to the ground. We also think, in a few cases, they've demanded more money before they let go."

Edna gasped, drawing Peg's and Ruther's attention. She shook her head to minimize her reaction. "I recently read about one of the cases. Wasn't it in or near Chicago--the trial in which the photojournalist Carol James was the primary witness?"

"That's right." The detective seemed satisfied with her explanation and turned back to Peg. "Mr. Bishop tells us that burning your house was only one of the threats he received. We're talking with Illinois officials and Treasury agents to verify the M.O., but we're pretty certain we're all dealing with the same guys. Your husband claims he was trying to save the bank and didn't know how else to put back the money in a way that wouldn't raise suspicions."

"And when both the fake and the real circle pins showed up, his duplicity was almost certain to surface," Edna speculated.

"That puzzles me," Peg said. "Why did he have a copy made of Mother's brooch when it wasn't among her jewels at the bank? It wasn't very clever of him."

"According to your husband, he found the design for the pin with a notation of the jeweler and the date it was given to your mother for her birthday." The detective picked up the little bag holding the original circle of precious stones and examined it. "It's a nice piece," he said before putting it back on the coffee table and looking up at Peg. "He thought you had it hidden away somewhere and that you would bring it out to wear sooner or later. He wanted to be ready with the copy, sure that this piece was one of the most valuable in the collection."

"How did it end up in the garden?" Edna thought back to the morning she'd spotted it gleaming in the sun. The thought also brought back a somewhat painful memory of getting her head stuck in the fence and, feeling a flush come to her cheeks, she pushed the memory away.

Speaking to Edna, Ruthers flicked his eyes toward Peg for an instant before explaining. "Mr. Bishop had it locked in his desk here at the house.

He thinks his wife has keys to both the office and the desk. He believes she found the pin and took it, but somehow lost it when she was working in the yard."

"That's ridiculous," Peg sat up with a snap at the accusation. "I have never had a key to my father's office or his desk and, if I had, I would never go through my husband's things." She scowled at the detective, shooting daggers at the messenger.

Edna reached over and patted Peg's forearm trying to reassure and calm her. "Would Virginia have gone into the office and rummaged in the desk?"

"That's a possibility, I suppose, although I don't know where she would have gotten a key. Besides, I've never known Virginia to go snooping around the house." Peg looked forlornly at Edna. "I guess we'll never know." Her look of desolation quickly turned to one of dread. "Do you suppose Stephen suspected her and killed her before she could expose him?"

Edna shook her head, speaking before Ruthers had a chance. "I don't think he had anything to do with Virginia's death." She gave Peg an apologetic look. "I admit that I've never been able to warm up to Stephen, but I don't think he'd plot to kill someone."

"What about last night," Peg insisted. "He seemed capable of killing *me*."

Edna turned to Ruthers. "What did he say about last night? Surely, you can tell us now."

"He says he had a blackout. Claims he

doesn't remember anything after wondering why his wife was in the attic so late at night." Ruthers raised his eyebrows. "When we tried to press him on that part of his story, he clammed up and wouldn't say any more without talking to his lawyer first."

"Convenient memory loss," Edna muttered more to herself than to the others, although her remark was loud enough for them to hear.

Ruthers looked at her with a mixture of curiosity and amusement. "What makes you think he wouldn't have poisoned Ms. Hoxie?"

"I don't think he'd have been that subtle," she replied. "And, I'd be very surprised if he knew anything about rosary peas, least of all that they are toxic. Besides, you said he thinks Peg took the brooch from his desk."

He nodded. "You're right. He's denying any knowledge of Ms. Hoxie's death, and I tend to believe him on that score. Her homicide is still an open case."

"Did he tell you what he's done with my mother's jewelry," Peg said. "He had copies made, but what happened to the real ones?"

"He gave them to a go-between. The courier delivers the goods and each piece is broken down so as not to be recognized. They probably melt the silver and gold and sell the metal separately from the gems."

Peg looked stricken. "They belonged to my mother and my grandmothers. Are you telling me they're all gone now? Destroyed?" Her voice rose and her eyes filled.

Ruthers spoke quickly, trying to reassure her and stem the flow of tears. "We don't know the extent yet. We have an expert examining everything that was in the safe deposit box. We'll give you her report in a day or two. We're guessing about what they've done with your jewelry, but haven't confirmed anything yet."

Edna felt her cheeks burn with anger over her friend's loss, but in the midst of it all, something was beginning to nag at her subconscious. "Did Stephen identify the courier, the one who received Peg's jewelry," she asked Ruthers.

He nodded. "Says it's the gardener. Goran Pittlani."

Chapter Twenty-Two

"No!" Edna's hands flew to her mouth as if she could catch the single word. She felt a cold, hard lump in the pit of her stomach.

Goran's got Jaycee. Has he handed her over to his gangster bosses like he turned over Peg's jewelry? Surely, she wouldn't have gone willingly. But Charlie said the gunman wouldn't have come looking for her if he knew she was with Goran. I must speak with Charlie.

The thoughts flicked through her head in less than a second.

"Ed?" Peg's voice broke her train of thought. "What is it?"

Ignoring the question, Edna stood abruptly. "Excuse me, please. I must make a call." She hurried into the foyer where she stopped to collect herself. "I must tell Charlie," she muttered. Too many alarms had been raised by that one name. *Goran Pittlani.*

"Whatever's the matter?" Peg had followed Edna into the foyer and now came up beside her to put a hand on Edna's back and rub gently. "If you're upset about the jewelry, please don't be. I'll get over the loss. I valued them, yes, but they're only possessions, after all."

"Mrs. Davies?" Trailing the women out of the library, Detective Ruthers approached Edna on her other side, the question in his voice apparent on his face. He, too, wanted to know what had caused her to react so vehemently.

Edna forced herself to smile. Until she spoke with Charlie, she didn't want to say anything to this other policeman. She also didn't want to add to Peg's worries. With that thought, Edna willed herself to appear unconcerned.

"Absurd of me, really. I didn't mean to cause such a stir. It's only that I remembered something I forgot to tell my neighbor. The mention of the gardener brought it to mind." She stopped there, realizing the less she said, the better. Her excuse sounded weak, even to her own ears, but she looked up at the detective with wide and innocent eyes, she hoped. "If you'll excuse me, I'll just go upstairs and make my phone call."

The detective looked at her sternly for several interminable seconds as Edna stared back with her expression frozen in place. Finally, he broke the glare and looked down at the baggies in his hand. He'd obviously picked them up before leaving the library. Stuffing them into his pocket, he looked back at Edna and then at Peg. "Do you know where I can reach Mr. Pittlani?"

Peg shook her head. "I haven't seen him since ..." She hesitated, thinking back. "... since he came in for lunch on Wednesday, the day Virginia died."

"If he shows up or you hear from him, call me immediately. I don't need to tell you that he may be dangerous." He looked again from one to the other, making the request of them both before turning toward the front door.

Edna waited where she was while Peg

showed Ruthers out, but as soon as the door closed behind him, she spun and hurried up the stairs, calling over her shoulder, "I'll be down in a minute. I have to make a call."

In her bedroom, she closed the door and dialed Charlie's number. When he answered on the third ring, she told him what she had learned from Detective Ruthers. Although she explained about the jewelry and Goran Pittlani's involvement, she decided not to complicate matters by telling him about the scene in the attic, which would also mean explaining how Stephen Bishop had ended up in the hospital.

"Do you think Goran might have tricked Jaycee into going with him, so he could turn her over to his gang," she asked, ending her report. When Charlie didn't say anything right away, she prodded, trying to impress upon him the urgency she felt. "Jaycee testified against them. They'll kill her for that."

"I don't think Jaycee is in any immediate danger."

"Why not? Have you heard from her?" He spoke so confidently, she wanted to believe him, but she also needed proof.

"Not yet, but I'm sure we will very soon." There was a short pause on the line before he added, "Mary spotted your gunman in town. We're close to picking him up."

"Do you think he knows where Goran has taken Jaycee?" She refused to be comforted until she knew for certain the young woman was safe and sound.

"I told you before that I doubt the two men work together. Let's take one thing at a time, shall we? First we catch this guy, then we find out what he knows and who he's working for. After that, we can concentrate on finding your missing neighbor." Charlie paused and she could hear voices in the background. "Gotta go, Edna. I'll let you know when I have news." He ended the call before she could say another word.

Setting her phone on the bedside table, she went slowly back downstairs feeling more frustrated than before she'd spoken to Charlie. She'd learned nothing from him and had received very little comfort that they were any closer to finding out what had happened to Jaycee. She sighed. *At least I've passed on the information about Goran, for what it's worth.*

Peg had built up the fire and was pacing in front of the hearth, rubbing her upper arms as if she were cold, although the room was overly warm. She stopped and turned when Edna entered.

"Talk to me, Ed. Detective Ruthers' mention of Goran's name has unduly upset you for some reason. I think it's more than his being mixed up in this business with my jewelry."

Edna didn't answer immediately. She didn't want to add to the burdens Peg was already shouldering, so pushed her worries for Jaycee to the back of her mind for the time being. "Weren't you surprised to learn that he conspired in these threats against Stephen?"

Without hesitation, Peg said, "I certainly was. I still find it hard to believe. He seemed so kind, gentle even."

"His being an imposter helps to explain why he knew so little about gardening," Edna said, then asked, "Did you ever see him lose his temper or act violent in any way?"

Peg paused, looking down into the fire for several seconds before lifting her chin and answering decisively, "Never. He was always cheerful and often considerate, doing small favors, particularly for Virginia." At the mention of her housekeeper's name, Peg gasped and her eyes widened. "Do you think Virginia found out what Goran was doing, and he killed her to keep her quiet?"

Edna shook her head. "Why would he use such a slow and uncertain method? If he wanted to silence her, he would have done it quickly." She refrained from describing the methods that came to mind. Instead, she stood beside Peg and stared into the fire. The flames were mesmerizing, helping her to relax and consider what she knew and what she had just learned that afternoon.

"What are you thinking?" Peg had turned her back to the fire, holding her hands behind her to warm them while she studied Edna with sad, blue-gray eyes.

"I'm wondering about the way Virginia died," Edna replied. "I can't quite put my finger on what's gnawing at me, but something I saw in her rooms is tickling my mind. There's a clue up there, but it's staying just outside my grasp."

After another moment's silence, Peg spoke with forced enthusiasm. "Let's take a break from the gloom in this old house and go for a walk. It's a nice day and the fresh air will do us both good. Maybe the exercise will help to jog loose whatever is stuck in your head."

For the next hour, the two friends strolled around the neighborhood and through the Brown University campus. Starting out, they'd made a pact to avoid any mention of Stephen's behavior or Virginia's death or Goran's complicity. They spoke of family matters, bringing each other up to date on the activities and accomplishments of their grandchildren and, eventually, found themselves back at the house.

Peg suggested an early, simple supper. Over a cup of hot tomato soup and a scoop of chicken salad on lettuce, she and Edna talked about what needed to be done by Sunday noon. With all that had happened, they'd lost a full day. They'd be twice as busy tomorrow with preparations for Virginia's memorial service.

"Besides Janette and her husband, will any other relatives be coming to the service," Edna asked after taking a sip of tea and setting down her cup.

Peg shook her head. "Janette has a son and two daughters, all married with children and grandchildren. The daughters, Virginia's nieces, are organizing a graveside service for the family in New Hampshire where Virginia will be buried next to her parents." Tears sprang into Peg's eyes, and she stopped talking.

Edna spoke to give Peg time to regain her composure. "On the drive here, Starling said to tell you she'll drive down from Boston. If we need her for anything last minute, I can call her tomorrow or early Sunday morning."

"Geoff and Kadie will come, but not their children," Peg said, referring to her son and daughter-in-law.

Edna thought of the television shows she'd watched where they mention the murderer always shows up at the victim's funeral. "I expect Detective Ruthers will want to be here."

Peg frowned. "Do you really think so?"

Edna shrugged. "No harm in inviting him officially, but I bet he's already planning on coming."

Once the supper dishes had been cleared away, the women decided to go to bed early and leave everything until the next day. Both were exhausted from the previous evening, and Edna found the afternoon's walk had relaxed her sufficiently to ensure a good night's sleep. In her room, she decided to phone Albert before crawling into bed.

"Looks like we'll be able to keep to our Sunday schedule," he reported. "We'll check out of the condo and head for home as early as we can. I've rented a car to drive Bea and Stan, so he'll have enough room to stretch out. George and Arthur will follow us in George's SUV. Stan's doing okay, but we'll stop fairly often along the way to let him walk around. I probably won't get home until late Sunday afternoon."

"That's wonderful, dear. It will be good to see you," she lied.

Ending the call with wishes for a safe trip and words of love, Edna felt her heart thudding in her chest. *What if Charlie doesn't catch the gunman before Albert gets home? Would Albert challenge a man with a gun if the thug got into the house again? How do I tell him the danger is thanks to our new neighbor who happens to be missing at the moment, along with Peg's gardener who isn't a gardener at all? And wait until Albert learns I put Peg's husband in the hospital.*

She almost laughed aloud at this last thought, but when the realization hit that they might all be in danger from unknown criminals, she tossed and turned for another hour before she was able to sleep.

Chapter Twenty-Three

Saturday morning Edna woke and dressed early only to find Peg already in the kitchen making coffee. She looked more rested than she had the day before.

"Sleep well?" Peg handed Edna a mug of coffee.

"Fitfully," Edna admitted, "but well enough. How about you?"

"I think I've found the perfect sleep remedy in that hot toddy of yours."

Edna laughed, and the women set about making a hearty breakfast while they chatted cheerily. Edna suspected Peg was acting happier than she felt, as was Edna herself. She smiled inwardly, thinking how nice it was to have such a friend. She rummaged in the refrigerator to find onions, green peppers and mushrooms, while Peg whipped up eggs with a little milk. Peg made the veggie omelet. Edna grated cheddar cheese and toasted English muffins.

They had only that day and the next morning to prepare the house and finish organizing Virginia's belongings, so after breakfast, they agreed on what needed to be done and what could be ignored if they ran out of time. Neither of them wanted to go into the attic, so Peg decided to put it off. She thought if she ever felt like exploring the upper regions again and found anything belonging to Virginia, she could deliver it to the relatives in New Hampshire at that time. She could probably talk Geoff into driving with her, if necessary. That decided, they got to work.

As Edna dusted and polished furniture, her mind churned away at the questions for which she so desperately wanted answers. *Where were Goran and Jaycee? Has he harmed her? Who poisoned Virginia?* Frustratingly, the answer to this last question hovered just out of reach of her consciousness.

Shortly before one o'clock, she finished cleaning the small bathroom off the back entryway. Still pondering the manner of Virginia's death, she was staring up the back stairwell when she heard Peg call from the kitchen.

"Ready for lunch?"

"Be right there," Edna called back, setting aside her pail and mop.

Peg had made tea, grilled cheese sandwiches and chocolate chip cookies which they ate at the kitchen table while comparing notes on what was still left to be done in preparation for the next day's memorial service.

"I need to get flowers," Peg said, about to rise and clear away the dishes. "Want to come with me?"

Edna shook her head, following Peg to the sink with her own cup and plate. "Unless you need my help, I thought I'd finish up in Virginia's rooms. There's not much left to do, but I want to go through the drawers and closets once more to make sure we didn't miss anything. Then a quick vacuum and dusting."

"Do you really want to do that by yourself? If you wait until I get back with the flowers ..."

Interrupting, Edna shook her head. "I can handle it in no time. Probably will be done before you get home, so then I can help you with floral arrangements." She wanted to spend time alone in Virginia's rooms and knew Peg would be a distraction. To give herself more time, she grinned at Peg and said, "Why don't you pick up a movie while you're out ... and popcorn, unless you have some in the house. We could do with some fun tonight."

"That's a great idea." Peg grinned back and left to run her errands.

Upstairs, Edna walked around the bedroom, sitting room and bathroom. Clothes, books and most of the knick-knacks had been boxed up and carefully labeled. The framed photographs had been left on the table so Virginia's sister Janette could select the ones she'd like to keep. Edna again studied the picture of Virginia with Renee and Cherisse Froissard, taken during their Florida vacation. She wondered if Renee would like it and set the picture beside the potted jade plant.

Her next chore was to pack up shoes and purses, all that were left in the closet. She then rechecked dresser drawers, closet shelves and, just to be certain, she got down on all fours and checked beneath the bed. When everything seemed to have been done, she stopped in the bathroom on her way to the sitting room. She opened the door to the linen closet and then turned to the medicine cabinet above the sink. It was full of bottles, cans and tubes.

Going down to the kitchen, she brought back several resealable plastic bags and began to sort through the cabinet shelves. She set one sack in the sink to hold whatever would be disposed of and filled it with an old tube of toothpaste, a bottle of aspirin that had passed the expiration date, a nearly-empty bottle of mouthwash, an old toothbrush and a comb. On the top shelf, she discovered an empty prescription bottle for Virginia's heart medication. From the date, she guessed that when Virginia had emptied it more than a year ago, she'd kept the empty container. Edna herself saved old bottles for reuse, particularly if they were clean and had tight lids. This one she held in her hand for a long moment, staring at the label. She assumed Virginia had still been on the medication and that the police had taken away the bottle that wasn't empty.

"That's it," she murmured. "It's the only thing that makes sense." She slipped the bottle into the pocket of her slacks and finished cleaning out Virginia's medicine cabinet with renewed energy.

When Peg got home, Edna didn't mention the prescription bottle which, by that time, was sitting on the dresser in her bedroom, waiting for the chance to show it to Detective Ruthers the following day. That evening, the two women had a pizza delivered and ate in front of the television, watching a Meryl Streep movie and sipping warm milk laced with brandy.

Chapter Twenty-Four

After breakfast on Sunday morning, Peg spread a white linen tablecloth over the dining room table and began to arrange china plates, crystal glasses, silverware and napkins. Flower arrangements from friends began to arrive, and Edna put them on tables around the foyer, library and living room. Peg had made a graceful arrangement of calla lilies in a clear-glass rectangular vase which Edna centered on the dining room table.

The day was cloudy and cool with the smell of rain in the air, although the forecast didn't call for precipitation. Edna filled the wood baskets in the library and living room, laying fires, ready to be lighted.

Virginia's sister Janette and her husband arrived shortly after noon and were soon followed by guests carrying dishes of finger sandwiches, raw vegetables, cookies and tiny cakes. Detective Ruthers showed up looking properly somber in a charcoal gray suit. Before Edna could close the door behind him, Starling came running up to the house and slipped inside, giving her mother a quick hug.

"Sorry I couldn't get here earlier," she said, shrugging out of her coat. "What can I do to help?"

The downstairs looked festive, but the

mood was solemn. Renee and Guy Froissard were the last to appear at a quarter to one. Peg had begun to show signs of impatience since the priest wanted to begin at half past noon. He'd have to leave by one to perform a wedding ceremony later that afternoon. Shortly after the service was supposed to start, Peg told Edna she'd delay ten minutes more because she didn't want to begin without Virginia's best friends present, and she also didn't want to offend Renee and Guy after her recent and tenuous reconciliation with them. Edna had a different reason for being anxious to see the brother and sister, and she was beginning to wonder if they would make it when they finally did walk through the front door.

Peg visibly relaxed. The service began and went smoothly. Guy was the last to speak, bringing tears to eyes and laughter to lips as he told a few stories of their friendship with the deceased. Edna was surprised that Renee didn't get up to say a few words, but thought Virginia's closest friend might be too emotional to speak without breaking down. Edna was keeping an eye on the woman, waiting for the opportunity to speak to her alone. It was very important that she do so.

When the service ended nearly fifteen minutes later than expected, the priest rushed off with apologies and the rest of the guests milled around the dining room table. Most wandered into the library or the living room where Edna had asked Starling to light the fires. People sat eating and talking quietly in small groups while a few men stayed in the dining room, picking food from serving trays instead of opting for a plate.

Busy being backup hostess for Peg, Edna lost track of Renee until, as she was removing an empty tray from the table, she looked up to see Cherisse's daughter disappear into the kitchen. Here was her chance, but just as she started to follow the elusive woman, Edna was stopped by a chatty couple from the church who wanted to introduce themselves. Half of her attention was riveted on the doorway, waiting for Renee to reappear. When she was still in the kitchen after nearly ten minutes, Edna managed to shake herself free of the couple and go looking for Renee.

She wasn't in either the kitchen or the lavatory off the back room, so Edna opened the back door and looked out into the yard. A cool, damp wind was blowing and she didn't think Renee would have gone outside, but she wanted to make certain. She also thought Renee wouldn't leave without her brother. A short time before, Edna had noticed Guy in the dining room speaking animatedly to an attractive, middle-aged woman. Having checked all other possibilities, Edna looked up the stairs, certain now where she would find Renee. *Perfect*, she thought.

Rather than climb the back stairs to Virginia's rooms, Edna went in search of Detective Ruthers and found him in the library, standing near the fireplace with Starling. Interrupting their conversation and asking her daughter to excuse them for a minute, Edna pulled Ruthers a few feet away and spoke quietly.

"I'd like you to come up to Virginia's sitting room in five minutes. No sooner, please. Give me five minutes."

He frowned down at her. "What's going on?"

"I believe this is the key," she said, removing the prescription bottle from her skirt pocket and handing it to him. "You'll see. Come up by the front stairs. Five minutes," she reminded him before leaving the room and moving swiftly up the grand staircase.

Treading softly, Edna approached the sitting room and peered around the half-opened door. Renee was standing next to the table that held the jade plant and the framed photographs that had not yet been packed away. Her back was to the hall entrance.

Taking a steadying breath, Edna pushed the door all the way open and strode into the room. "Hello, Renee."

The woman spun around, dropping the picture she'd been holding. Fortunately, the frame landed on the rug, silently and unbroken.

Edna picked it up as Renee stood, still surprised and looking guilty. She'd been crying, but not in the last several minutes.

"She was a good friend of yours, wasn't she?" Edna's question was rhetorical. The picture she held was the one taken of the three women in Florida.

Renee nodded, her eyes fixed on Edna's face. Her expression had turned to one of curious impatience, but she didn't speak.

"You must have known about her weak heart," Edna said.

"I did," Renee acknowledged, frowning. "What of it?" She probably meant to sound casually indifferent, but her words held no conviction.

Edna raised her eyebrows, expressing her surprise. "You were a trained nurse. You must have known a shock to Virginia's system could precipitate a heart attack."

Indignantly, Renee retorted, "What are you talking about." Her words were harsh, but not convincing.

"You're the one who cut the rosary pea and put it into Virginia's food."

For a long minute they stared at each other and Edna was beginning to think Renee wouldn't confess when the woman seemed to shrink before collapsing onto a hard-backed chair set beside the table.

Looking away from Edna, Renee said, "What makes you so sure?"

Placing the picture back on the table next to the jade plant, Edna pulled the other straight chair forward so she could sit facing Renee. Half turned toward the hallway door, Edna caught a slight movement. She didn't look in his direction but knew Ruthers was standing just outside. In a slightly louder voice, she said, "When I started putting the pieces together, you were the only one who made sense. You garden, so you know about plants. You gave the rosary to Virginia, and you knew about her heart condition. What I don't understand is 'why.' What did you have to gain by killing your friend?"

"She betrayed our friendship." Renee's head jerked up and her eyes flashed. "If she had been a true friend, she wouldn't have taken the brooch from Mama."

"You killed her because she took a pin?" Edna's words reflected the incredulity she felt as her own anger began to rise.

Renee shook her head and seemed to deflate before Edna's eyes. "I didn't mean for her to die. It was an accident. I had no idea she had been handling the beads as much as she was and that so much poison had already gotten into her system. That, on top of her heart condition ..." Renee paused and drew in a shaky breath before continuing. "She shouldn't have died. That single seed was only supposed to make her sick. I would come to tend her. When she slept, I could search her room and get Mama's brooch back." Renee's words were fading as she bowed her head, repeating, "It was a mistake. She wasn't supposed to die."

Edna nodded. "I thought that's what must have happened when I cleaned out the medicine cabinet and found her prescription bottle. If she was taking such a strong dose, her heart would have been too weak to stand the severity of the attack caused by the abrin poison."

"I didn't realize her heart condition had gotten worse, but she upset Mama. I was so mad at her and only wanted to get the brooch back." Renee hadn't raised her head, but Edna could see tears beginning to trickle down her cheeks.

At that moment she was aware of Ruthers moving up quietly to stand beside Renee. When he put a hand on the woman's shoulder, she started and looked up. After several seconds during which she looked as though she were trying to figure out who he was and where he'd come from, she spoke defiantly. "Mama earned that brooch. She was so obsessed with the colors of France, she paid with her reputation. Virginia had no right to take it from her."

Putting her bowed head in both hands, Renee began to sob. Before Edna or Ruthers could react, Guy burst from the bathroom and rushed to his sister's side. He must have come up the back stairs, Edna thought as he knelt between their chairs and took Renee into his arms.

"What have you done? What have you done," he repeated over and over as he rocked her gently.

Ruthers removed his hand from Renee's shoulder and held it out to Edna. Helping her to rise from the chair, he said quietly, "I'll have to take her in and get her booked. Please inform Mrs. Bishop that I've left with the Froissards. Nothing more, just that. If she asks, tell her I'll be back shortly to speak with her and Ms. Hoxie's relatives." He paused a moment before adding, "I think that's all for now."

The detective turned to Guy. "She'll have to come with me, but you may follow us, if you wish. I suggest you have your lawyer meet us at Division headquarters."

Guy nodded, rising to help his sister to her feet.

Ruthers ushered the Froissards toward the back stairs. Guy walked beside Renee, one arm around her waist as she leaned against him. Edna followed the trio down the back stairs. She wanted to be less conspicuous entering the dining room from the kitchen rather than walking down the stairs into the foyer.

When she reached the kitchen, she found Starling loading glasses and plates into the dishwasher. To her daughter's startled and questioning look, she said, "I'll explain later, dear," and went through the room in search of Peg.

Within the next twenty minutes, guests began to leave and a half hour later only a few family and friends remained. Peg showed Janette and her husband upstairs where they began to sort through the labeled boxes. Geoff Luccianello, his wife and Starling helped carry cartons down to the couple's Chevy Suburban. Edna packed the final items that Janette wanted while Peg boxed up what little remained for delivery to the Goodwill center.

When the last box had been closed, Edna went downstairs to finish cleaning up. The dishes were done, chairs moved back and all the cartons loaded into the SUV by the time Detective Ruthers returned. When he suggested everyone gather in the library, Edna quietly begged off. She was exhausted and hoped to get home before Albert.

"We're not needed here and will only be in

the way," she said of herself and Starling. "You know where to reach me." When Ruthers agreed and disappeared into the library, Edna spoke to her daughter.

"You don't mind driving me home, do you, dear?"

"Is it safe? I haven't had time to call Charlie. Do you know if he's caught the gunman?"

"I don't, but I'm going home, regardless. Geoff has invited Peg to stay with them for a few days. She said she'd stay here with me if I wanted her to, but I said no. Your father will be home this afternoon, and I can't leave it to Charlie to explain why we must vacate the house."

Several minutes later, as Starling pulled away from the Graystocking home and headed for Interstate 95, she said, "Speaking of explaining things, what happened this afternoon?"

Only Peg had realized the implications when Edna told her about Renee's arrest and that Ruthers would explain everything. Peg had wanted details, of course, but Edna only shook her head.

"Detective Ruthers has more information than I, and he'll be back soon," was all she would say to either Peg or Starling who had also tried to pry information from her mother.

Now, as they drove south, Edna filled Starling in on events since they had parted company Thursday night. She began with the altercation in the attic and ended with Renee's confession.

"So it was all a horrible mistake. How tragic," Starling said, her voice filled with emotion. "What do you think will happen to Renee?"

Edna shook her head. "That's up to the lawyers and judges and, perhaps, a jury. Her nightmare is just beginning, I'm afraid."

"You said her mother's in a nursing home and not very strong. What will this do to her?"

"Hard to say, dear. She has her son to lean on, and sometimes a mother will rally, gain unimaginable strength when her child is in trouble." She smiled at her daughter's profile, wondering if there were anything she wouldn't do for her own children.

Keeping her eyes on the road, Starling was silent for a moment before she asked hesitantly, "Do you think Aunt Peg will divorce Stephen?"

Edna didn't need to think before replying, "I certainly hope so. I can't see how she could ever trust him again, after what he's done." She sighed. "But I've learned never to second guess anyone." She paused before adding, mostly to herself, "Whatever happens, the immediate future does not look good for my dear old friend."

They were both silent as Starling maneuvered the car to the left lanes and merged toward Route 1. Settling back into the stream of traffic, she said, "You think Dad's home by now?"

Edna felt her stomach lurch at the thought of Albert arriving home and running into a gunman lurking around the house or, worse yet, hiding inside the house. *If Mary hadn't taken that memory chip from Jaycee's envelope, I wouldn't need to worry.* She felt more than a twinge of anger at her neighbor's meddling ways before remembering how Mary's curiosity and interference had once saved her life.

"Are you going to tell Dad about this one," Starling asked, as if reading Edna's mind. "You've now been involved with, what, three murders, and he doesn't know about any of them."

"It's not that I haven't wanted to tell him," Edna said defensively. "By the time he was around for me to explain, everything was all over, all wrapped up."

"Not this time," Starling said. "Not unless Charlie has found your intruder. Do you think the guy's dumb enough to hang around or arrogant enough to think he won't get caught?"

"I haven't a clue." Edna's head was beginning to throb. Starling had brought up questions Edna would just as soon ignore, but knew she couldn't.

Chapter Twenty-Five

When Starling turned into the driveway, Edna saw Charlie's car parked behind hers in front of the house. He was standing beside her dark blue sedan, talking to Mary and stroking Benjamin who lay on the Buick's hood. Wearing her favorite jungle fatigues, Mary was cradling a small black cat in her arms while Hank sat on his haunches staring up at her. Edna's hopes soared at the calm, almost happy, scene which boded good news.

She jumped from the car almost before Starling had time to turn off the engine. Starling leaped out, too, and they both rushed up to the pair.

"Have you caught him," Edna asked Charlie.

"Did Jaycee get home," Starling said at the same time.

Charlie raised his arms as if fending off an attack. Only Edna's subconscious recorded the startled kitten bounding from Mary's grasp and disappearing around the corner of the house with Benjamin close behind.

"One thing at a time," Charlie said, putting an arm around Starling's shoulders as she nestled into his side. He looked at Edna. "Yes, we've arrested the man who threatened you. Mary's sighting proved out and he's safely locked away. Chicago police have been looking for him, too. They're sending a man to escort the prisoner home. Their charges are more serious than ours."

"What about Jaycee? Have you heard from her?" Starling repeated her earlier question impatiently.

Before anyone could answer, the sound of a car crunching on broken shells made them all turn to see a red Kia pull up and stop behind Starling's Toyota. Having expected to see Albert, Edna was puzzled at who would be visiting on this Sunday afternoon until she saw Goran and Jaycee alight.

She gasped and turned to Charlie. "Arrest him," she blurted, so astonished was she to finally see the man who had been on her mind for the past several days.

"Whoa," Charlie said, a mischievous twinkle in his eye. "I have no authority to arrest a special agent."

The newcomers strolled up to join the group. Goran's smile was cocky. Jaycee looked relaxed and happy.

Edna was speechless, busy absorbing what Charlie had just said. "Special agent?"

"Yes, ma'am. Treasury. At your service," Goran bowed from the waist before nodding an acknowledgement to Charlie.

Edna narrowed her eyes at him while the puzzle pieces inside her head began to fall into place and form a recognizable picture. She turned accusingly to Charlie. "You knew about Goran? Why didn't you tell me?"

Charlie looked both surprised and innocence. "Only since Thursday afternoon. My captain called me in. Said I should stop asking questions about a case that didn't belong to me." He shrugged. "I made an educated guess. Even if I'd been certain, I can't divulge information in an ongoing investigation." He gave her his crooked smile. "I did tell you not to worry."

Edna turned back to Goran, voicing her thoughts as, one by one, events started to make sense. "You're on the case involving threats to bankers," she said, flicking her eyes toward Jaycee, "The same one Carol James accidently got mixed up in."

Goran smiled at Jaycee before returning Edna's gaze. "I recognized her from our file photos when I drove up to your house that day. You could have pushed me over with a straw, but I couldn't let on. It would have blown my cover."

"Your cover as a gardener was so you could watch Stephen Bishop," Edna said. He nodded and was about to speak, but she cut him off. "Did he know you were watching him?"

Goran shook his head. "We couldn't trust him not to give away the operation. He had to be kept in the dark."

"How did you get him to hire you?"

"That was pure coincidence. We'd already contacted the lawn maintenance company the Bishops use. They'd already agreed to send me in as an employee, and when Bishop mentioned his wife wanted to restore the gardens, it was just the excuse I needed to hang around the place."

Mary, Charlie and Starling were listening to Edna and Goran with rapt attention. Besides

Goran, only Edna had known that Stephen Bishop was one of the bankers being threatened. She was also the only one who knew of his duplicity in stealing his wife's jewelry in order to pay off the extortionists.

Remembering Stephen's suspicions that Peg had been in his office, Edna said, "You were the one who took the brooch from Stephen's desk."

"Right again," Goran agreed. "I broke into the office one afternoon when nobody was home. Easy enough since I had access to the house. We're bonded, you know." He gave a short laugh at his own joke before he went on. "I thought something funny must be going on when Bishop was so ready to give up his wife's jewelry, once he'd depleted his own savings. I'd already decided to go through his desk to see if there was anything pertinent to our investigation. When I saw the brooch, I took it to have it appraised. I'd planned to put it back before he could miss it."

"Did you know it was a copy?"

He shook his head, "I suspected, but didn't know for sure."

"How did it end up in the dirt," Starling spoke up. "Mother told me that's where she found it."

He looked sheepish. "Careless of me. It must have dropped out of my pocket when I was tilling up the garden, probably when I pulled out my handkerchief to wipe my face. I didn't have a clue where to look when I realized it was gone." His voice was full of suppressed laughter when he said, "Nice of your mother to find it and hang around until I got there."

Edna felt the color creep up her neck and into her cheeks at the memory of getting caught in the fence. She quickly diverted the conversation. "Stephen thought Peg took the brooch from his desk. Why didn't he suspect you, since you were the one receiving his payments?"

"Remember. He knew me only as a gardener," Goran said. "His payoffs were left at a drop sight. Bishop never dealt directly with anyone except the initial contact and that was necessary only to acquire the original loan. After that, Bishop received his instructions by phone."

"How did *you* know where the drop was, then?" This time Mary asked the question. Edna was surprised her crime-enthusiast neighbor had managed to keep quiet for as long as she had.

"I was informed through my contact at the Treasury," Goran said. He winked at Mary and added, "Can't tell you how they found out. Top secret."

"What did you do with the jewelry," Edna said with the sudden realization that Peg might be able to reclaim some of her property if it hadn't, in fact, been turned over to be broken apart or melted down.

Goran's eyes sparkled with suppressed humor. "Every piece is tucked away in a safe deposit box at her husband's bank."

Edna stood stunned for a second or two before she choked out a laugh. "You're kidding. You hid it right under Stephen's nose?"

"Sure did. Made certain he wasn't around when I went to the vault, of course, but I figured it would be a pretty safe place."

They all laughed, and Edna shook her head, chuckling at his audacity. "Peg will be pleased and relieved."

Starling turned to Jaycee. "Where have you been? We were worried about you."

The young woman frowned and looked from Starling to Edna. "Didn't you get my note? I stuck it on your front door."

"It ended up under our wet newspaper," Edna explained, "looking more like a finger painting than a message."

"What did it say," Starling asked.

"I wrote that Goran and I would be away for a few days and please don't worry." Jaycee looked apologetically at Starling. "I know we had plans. I'm so sorry you didn't get my message."

Uncharacteristically, Starling didn't seem in a forgiving mood, at the moment. "Why did you leave that envelope with my mother? She and Mary were threatened as a result of your thoughtlessness. They could have been killed."

"I know, I know," Jaycee said, obviously upset at both the thought and the accusation. "When Goran came to my house to tell me who he was and that my cover had been blown, we had to leave at once. It was the middle of the night. I didn't have a chance to get the envelope back, and I really didn't think anyone would suspect your mother was holding it for me."

Edna interjected to calm her daughter. "It

wasn't Jaycee's fault. That man wouldn't have known if I hadn't answered the door with the envelope in my hand." To Jaycee and Goran, she said, "Where *have* you been?"

"Hopping around Boston suburbs," Goran answered. "We stayed in a different town each night and roamed around during the day." He glanced at Jaycee with affection.

"Were you hiding from the guy in the picture, the shadow guy," Mary asked. "Is that who we just arrested?"

"From what I learned this afternoon, our lab techs are nearly positive the shadow in the photo matches the profile of the man you arrested," Goran answered Mary, speaking to Charlie as well.

Jaycee said. "I didn't realize that the fire was all part of this major extortion ring until after I agreed to testify. I received several threats before the trial, but once it was over and the arsonist went to prison, I thought it was all over."

Goran picked up the explanation. "We'd been watching this bunch, building a case. When Carol ... or Jaycee ..." he stopped and shrugged. "To avoid confusing everyone, let's keep calling her Jaycee. Anyway, when she left Chicago and went to stay with her grandmother in Florida, everyone thought she was out of harm's way. I wasn't really part of that end of things, just assigned here in Providence to watch Bishop, once we took out the real courier. You could have blown me away when I met up with one of our chief witnesses right here in this yard.

"When I notified my superiors that Carol James was in the area, they told me to get her out. Said they'd just learned she'd been located. My cover was established at the Bishop's and things were pretty quiet, so her safety became my top priority." He grinned at her. "Best assignment of my career." She reddened slightly and smiled back.

"If you were safe in Florida, how come you came up here," Mary asked. She had been quiet, watching and listening carefully to all that was said. As usual, her question was pertinent, if not diplomatic.

Jaycee met Mary's steady gaze. "When I found evidence of a second man at the fire, I figured they'd still be after me. I had already hoped to spend some time here in New England, so I just left Florida sooner than planned. I didn't want Gran to get involved."

"Hadn't you spotted the shadow man in your pictures before you testified," Starling asked, using Mary's name for the arsonist.

Jaycee shook her head. "I got the memory chip back only after the trial was over. When I got to Gran's, I was showing the pictures to her and that's when I saw him. She was sitting at the computer and I was standing behind her. When seen from a distance, it's a more obvious silhouette. I called Dietz to tell him what I found. He was my contact in Chicago."

Edna studied Jaycee for a second or two and said, "We guessed why someone was after you when we saw that shadow in your photos and realized you had proof of a second arsonist. It explains why you're using an alias, but why did your grandmother buy a house? Why not just rent an apartment?"

"That was Gran's idea when I told her why I had to leave for a while. She insisted on talking to Dietz and when she found out he had a contact not far from Westerly where she'd grown up, she insisted I come here. She thought if she bought a house under her name, nobody would guess this is where I'd be staying. Besides, we didn't know how long I'd have to hide out." A blush reddened her cheeks. "Guess we have a lot to learn about going underground."

Charlie frowned peevishly. "I wish Dietz had filled me in more before he went off on another assignment. It's a good think Goran happened along and knew enough to take over."

Mary uncrossed her arms and rested her hands behind her, as if she were about to boost herself onto the hood of the car. She asked Jaycee, "Will you sell and move away now?"

Their neighbor shook her head and flushed with pleasure. "Actually, no. My idea for an illustrated, historic cookbook is something I want to pursue. At first, Gran and I thought it up as a cover story, but after we talked about it and you all had such great ideas," at this she looked from Mary to Edna to Starling, "I'm hooked--on the food and on all the history in this region. Also, Gran wants to come for a visit, back to her old 'stompin' ground,' as she calls it. Actually, I think that's why she bought the house in the first place."

"So, you won't disappear on us again," Edna asked with a smile.

"Well, maybe once in a while," Jaycee admitted. She grinned up at Goran and slipped her hand into his.

"She'll be needed in Chicago," he said, "while we're tying up the case." He looked at Charlie. "She's in no more danger, since you arrested the second arsonist and Chicago's got the head of this little organization. This time, we've got plenty of witnesses who've agreed to testify. That's taken some of the attention off Jaycee, too."

With a sudden thought, Edna said, "What about the Providence police? According to them, you're one of the extortionists. They're looking for you."

"Not any more," Charlie interjected. "I phoned the department this afternoon. Talked to a detective working on the case and told her that Pittlani and I would be in to talk with them sometime tomorrow."

"Is that your real name? Goran Pittlani?" Mary asked.

"Don't you like it," Goran tried to look offended, but there was a twinkle in his eye. He didn't answer her question, though, before Starling spoke up.

"Getting back to the idea of food," she said, nodding at Jaycee. "I'm starving. Does anyone else want to go eat?" She looked around the group.

"Sounds like a good idea to me," Charlie

said. He also looked around to include everyone when he added, "Anyone up for a little surf and turf?"

"I need to find my kitten and feed Hank," Mary said, pushing away from the car. "Thanks all the same."

Edna glanced at her watch. "I want to be here when Albert gets home, so I'll pass, too. You young folks go along."

Mary strode off toward her house with Hank running ahead of her. Charlie opened the door of his car for Starling, and Goran put his arm around Jaycee's shoulders as they headed for the Kia. Edna retrieved her suitcase from Starling's car and, as she unlocked and opened the front door, Benjamin scampered in. Before she stepped inside, Edna waved to Mary when her neighbor turned to call to the half-grown, black kitten who was cautiously stalking her.

While Edna unpacked her bag, fed Benjamin and prepared a supper that could be heated quickly once Albert arrived, she mulled over what she could tell him about the past week. While he had been away, tending to Stan instead of enjoying a relaxing week of golf, she had spent most of her time with Peg.

Edna would, of course, tell Albert about Virginia's death, although the complication of the brooch and how she happened to spot it or the Froissard family's involvement were all irrelevant. No, she wouldn't tire Albert with insignificant details. After all, he had not known Virginia well, had not known the Froissards at all, and wasn't interested in jewelry.

She was certain he would like to know that Stephen Bishop was in the hospital recovering from knee surgery and that Peg would probably be getting a divorce, but he needn't be concerned with the how's or why's.

Breaking lettuce into a small bowl, ready to be dressed before dinner, she wondered what to tell Albert about their new neighbor. That she was young and pretty, certainly, and that she was a photojournalist. He would like the fact that Jaycee had so much in common with their youngest daughter. Edna wouldn't mention being threatened at gunpoint. It would only cause Albert undue distress and he'd had enough worries this past week. If pieces of Jaycee's history came into conversation in the future which might prompt him to ask questions, she would explain then. She really doubted her possession of Jaycee's camera chip would arise.

With a self-satisfied sigh, she thought the summary of her week would please and entertain Albert while they enjoyed their usual pre-dinner drink by the fire.

An hour later, she was sitting in her favorite chair beside a glowing fire, listening to her "Middlemarch" audio book and working on the sweater for her six-month-old grandson when Albert got home.

# # #

Acknowledgements

A particular "thank you" goes to my cousin for his real estate expertise and for the guided tour of Martha's Vineyard.

As always, I am indebted to Jim Coleman, Olivia Coleman, Lori Gee, Gail Lindsey and Jan Reynolds for their expertise and feedback as first readers.

I especially wish to acknowledge my critic group members Bonnie McCune and Elizabeth Cook for their support, guidance and insights. You're the best!

To my generous and talented friend Sandi Marsh, thank you for my web site: www.SuzanneYoungBooks.com.

Thank you, Jamie Reddig, for your wonderful artistic flair.

And to my family, friends and readers who have been so supportive and encouraging: You make my efforts fun and worthwhile. Many thanks!

About the Author

Suzanne Young was born and raised in Rhode Island. She has worked as a writer, an editor and a computer programmer since earning her degree in English from the University of Rhode Island in Kingston.

A resident of Colorado for over 40 years, she retired from software development in 2010 to write fiction full time.

She is a member of Denver Woman's Press Club, Rocky Mountain Fiction Writers, Sisters in Crime and Mystery Writers of America, as well as a graduate of the Arvada (CO) Citizens Police Academy.

To learn more about this author, she invites you to visit her website at www.SuzanneYoungBooks.com where you may also contact her via e-mail.

Made in the USA
San Bernardino, CA
03 July 2015